A blast of explosives smashed the embassy's security fence

The gate collapsed in a heap of tangled bars and concrete dust. Valdez and his terrorists returned to the threshold and continued the assault on the embassy, spraying the compound with automatic-weapons fire. A pair of gunners spotted Mack Bolan and fired on his position.

The Executioner jacked the pump Remington as he ducked for cover behind a parked Chevy. A volley of gunfire chased the warrior, slugs punching a line of holes in the bodywork. He whipped the shotgun's barrel across the hood and fired the weapon without aiming, not expecting to score a hit, intending only to keep the enemy at bay.

He stayed low and moved along the length of the vehicle, risking a look from his new position as he drew the Desert Eagle. A shooter staggered on unsteady legs, peppered by pellet wounds. A quick shot from the big .44 took him out of play.

The second terrorist whirled and swung his weapon toward the Executioner, who triggered the Desert Eagle twice. Both .44 slugs drilled the gunner in the center of his chest, the impacts hurling him to the ground.

Bolan scanned the area, searching for his primary target. The grenade launcher lay on the pavement, but Adolfo Valdez was nowhere to be seen.

MACK BOLAN ®

The Executioner

DON PENDLETON'S
THE EXECUTIONER®
COMBAT ZONE

A GOLD EAGLE BOOK FROM
WORLDWIDE®

TORONTO • NEW YORK • LONDON
AMSTERDAM • PARIS • SYDNEY • HAMBURG
STOCKHOLM • ATHENS • TOKYO • MILAN
MADRID • WARSAW • BUDAPEST • AUCKLAND

First edition October 1995

ISBN 0-373-64202-4

Special thanks and acknowledgment to
William Fieldhouse for his contribution to this work.

COMBAT ZONE

Land and Liberty, and Death to the Rich Land Owners!
—Emiliano Zapata

People everywhere should have freedom, and some
governments need to be toppled. Sometimes armed force
is the only way to achieve social change.
—Mack Bolan

THE
MACK BOLAN®
LEGEND

Nothing less than a war could have fashioned the destiny of the man called Mack Bolan. Bolan earned the Executioner title in the jungle hell of Vietnam.

But this soldier also wore another name—Sergeant Mercy. He was so tagged because of the compassion he showed to wounded comrades-in-arms and Vietnamese civilians.

Mack Bolan's second tour of duty ended prematurely when he was given emergency leave to return home and bury his family, victims of the Mob. Then he declared a one-man war against the Mafia.

He confronted the Families head-on from coast to coast, and soon a hope of victory began to appear. But Bolan had broken society's every rule. That same society started gunning for this elusive warrior—to no avail.

So Bolan was offered amnesty to work within the system against terrorism. This time, as an employee of Uncle Sam, Bolan became Colonel John Phoenix. With a command center at Stony Man Farm in Virginia, he and his new allies—Able Team and Phoenix Force—waged relentless war on a new adversary: the KGB.

But when his one true love, April Rose, died at the hands of the Soviet terror machine, Bolan severed all ties with Establishment authority.

Now, after a lengthy lone-wolf struggle and much soul-searching, the Executioner has agreed to enter an "arm's-length" alliance with his government once more, reserving the right to pursue personal missions in his Everlasting War.

PROLOGUE

Hal Brognola sat at the conference table in the War Room at Stony Man Farm. Stubble lined his jaw, dark circles traced his lower eyelids and his white dress shirt appeared wrinkled. The big Fed had endured yet another long, hard night, and probably a long, hard day before the all-nighter, Mack Bolan thought as he stood in the doorway.

"You look like you could do with some time off," Bolan remarked as he entered the room.

"Hello to you too, Striker."

"You ought to listen to him, Hal," Aaron Kurtzman urged. "I've been telling you the same thing for weeks. You need to get away from this for a while."

Kurtzman also sat at the table. The furniture concealed his wheelchair from Bolan's view. A bullet in the spine condemned the man to use a wheelchair for the rest of his life, yet he continued to command the Stony Man computer center.

"I'm touched by your concern," Brognola stated gruffly. "Now, let's get to work. I was in Washington yesterday and met with the President. He has a problem and he wants us to take care of it."

The Executioner took a seat across from the big Fed, and the man continued.

"The President talked about some recent events in Mexico. An American businessman named Brian Henderson was murdered in Mexico City. He and two other executives were heading for their limo when some guys disguised as road construction workers suddenly produced automatic weapons and opened fire. The hit team cut them down so fast nobody had a chance to duck for cover.

"The killers nailed Henderson in the lot in front of the Newton Manufacturing Corporation headquarters building. He was the top executive officer of the company in Mexico. They wanted to make sure everybody knew why he was killed. By the way, security officers rushed to the scene only to run into sniper fire. They got picked off like targets at a range. Then the killers made their escape before the local cops could arrive."

"Well executed," Bolan stated. "Sounds like they've been well trained and planned the hit with professional efficiency."

"Exactly," Brognola said. "Less than four hours later, the second hit occurred. Former U.S. Senator Gerald Corey was on vacation in Acapulco. He'd rented a small yacht to do some fishing. Two small motorboats suddenly closed in. They fired automatic rifles at Corey as he sat at the bow in a deck chair with a rod and reel in his hands. A Mexican national named Vargas was also on deck, fishing with Corey. Vargas owned a restaurant in Acapulco. Corey and he had been friends for years. Both men were hit by several rounds.

"Just to be sure, the terrorists fired two 40 mm grenade shells into the yacht. The explosions pretty much broke the craft in two. Corey's wife and two crew members were killed. Police patrol boats later found the speedboats used by the assassins, but the killers themselves had escaped. Another professional hit that displayed skill, daring and good planning."

"Somebody declared open season on VIPs from the United States," Bolan commented.

"And we've got an idea who it might be," Kurtzman declared. "Someone named Adolfo Valdez. Give a kid a name like that, and you're just asking for trouble. The guy's a second-generation Mexican American, born and raised in southern California. Did well in school, no evidence he got in any major trouble as a kid. Joined the U.S. Army when he was eighteen. Went Airborne and later Special Forces. Scored pretty high at just about everything. Weapons, hand-to-hand combat, strategy, escape and evasion, survival training and so on. Valdez seemed to have quite a career in the Army and received a promotion to staff sergeant less than a week before they sent him to Panama on December 20, 1989."

"Operation Just Cause."

"You guessed it," Brognola said. "Valdez seemed perfect for an assignment to Panama. In addition to his skills, he's bilingual and speaks Spanish as fluently as English. However, Operation Just Cause soon soured him on the U.S. military, our government and the United States in general. He decided those charges of 'Yankee imperialism' in Central and South America were more than just Commie banners. That invasion of Panama convinced him Uncle Sam was the bully on the block, ready and willing to crush any regime in Latin America that pissed off Washington.''

"After Panama Valdez stopped being a model soldier," Kurtzman said, picking up the story. "He became argumentative and disobeyed superiors on several occasions. Finally he lost his temper with an officer and beat the stuffings out of him. Damn near killed the guy. That incident led to a court martial, two years in prison and a dishonorable discharge.''

"Pretty sad end to military service that started so well," Bolan remarked. "How does Valdez play into these assassinations in Mexico?''

"When he got out of prison," Brognola replied, "Valdez moved on to a new career as a gunrunner, mostly smuggling U.S. military weapons stolen off the assembly line. It's no surprise that he specialized in running guns to Latin America. His favorite clients soon became certain militant branches of the Zapatistas.''

"Zapatista National Liberation Army," Kurtzman added. "You might recall they seized control of six cities in southeast Mexico on New Year's Day, January 1994. That's also the day the North American Free Trade Agreement officially began. The Zapatistas have made no secret of their opposition to NAFTA. They see it as a combined effort by the governments of

Mexico and the United States to further oppress the Indian peasant class.''

"Yeah," Bolan said. "I've read a little bit about them. I also recall the Zapatistas have their own leaders. A guy wearing a black ski mask called himself Subcomandante Marcos and occasionally spoke at press conferences on behalf of the rebels. Mostly he seemed to be demanding better housing, health care, schools and distribution of land for the Indians."

"This is different, Mack," Brognola stated. "Zapatista guerrillas have clashed with the Mexican military in the past. At least one hundred people were killed during the fighting in January 1994 before both sides agreed on a truce. But they never used the sort of tactics that are going on now. The Zapatistas haven't been accused of deliberate acts of murder or targeting U.S. citizens for assassination. That didn't happen until Valdez decided to move south of the border."

"The Justice Department had been putting together evidence to nail Valdez for gun smuggling," Kurtzman began. "The Bureau of Alcohol, Tobacco and Firearms had a pretty good idea who his accomplices were and the Feds were getting ready to toss the net when Valdez made a trip to Mexico City and didn't come back. A couple days after he left, folks showed up at his apartment to claim just about everything he left behind. They had signed receipts to prove they had paid for the stuff."

"Sort of a variation of a garage sale," Bolan stated. "Pretty slick. He must have suspected the Feds had him under surveillance. That still doesn't prove he's responsible for the murders of Henderson, Corey and the others.''

"No, it doesn't," Brognola agreed. "But you have to admit it's a hell of a coincidence Valdez just happens to move to Mexico and a few days later commando-style hit teams are taking out VIPs from the U.S.A.''

"We've got his file here," Kurtzman added. "It includes military background, prison record and personality evaluations by psychologists. His former patriotism has been replaced by anger, bitterness and a sense of betrayal. I think you'll agree the man is capable of something like this.''

"And frankly, that's one of the main reasons the President wants us to handle this," Brognola explained. "NAFTA is one of his pet projects. He and a lot of people in both political parties worked overtime to sell the policy to the American people. Of course there's still plenty of debate about whether this will cost jobs for folks in the U.S. or create employment due to increased trade with Mexico. I don't know one way or the other. We don't make policies at Stony Man. You know what we do here, Mack.''

"We don't help the President cover up embarrassments either," Bolan reminded him. "It won't be positive press if it becomes public knowledge a Mexican American became so soured against his own country he organized a bunch of fanatics to start killing U.S. citizens to protest NAFTA.''

The big Fed sighed. "The President doesn't expect us to cover up facts. If Valdez is behind this, the

Commander in Chief wants us to take care of the situation and the hell with how it looks. This really isn't about NAFTA anyway. Valdez has probably been looking for something he could use to put together a commando-style terrorist army to strike back at the U.S. somehow. What the President is concerned about is the possibility of security leaks putting out half-truths and wild rumors to the general public. He just wants all the facts in before any official statement is made. It would be even better if Valdez was under arrest at the time.''

"That's why we want this done with a small number of people aware of all the details," Kurtzman added. "You'll have a CIA contact at the embassy, but he won't know any more than we have to tell him. Basically he'll be your supply line for gear sent by diplomatic pouch. I've got a number of good choices among Mexican nationals who can work with you when you arrive. The best is a guy named Santos in Mexico City. All we need is for you to accept the mission and we'll get him for you.''

"Make the phone call, Bear, and I'll get my gear together.''

1

Mexico

Mack Bolan swiveled the tripod-mounted laser microphone and peered through the telescope sight. A casual observer might assume Bolan was a surveyor, measuring the distance from the hill to the Elizondo auto-repair shop five hundred yards away. But surveyors generally didn't work at one o'clock in the morning.

They usually didn't carry weapons, either. The Executioner was on a reconnaissance mission, but he had come prepared in case the probe turned hard. He carried a Beretta 93-R in shoulder leather, Ka-bar fighting knife in a belt sheath and a garrote in a jacket pocket. The warrior also packed spare magazines for the Beretta and several M-26 grenades. A Marlin .30-30 leaned on a tree trunk within easy reach.

Some sort of snag had occurred in Bolan's supply line. Somewhere between Stony Man Farm and the U.S. embassy in Mexico City delivery of his shipment was delayed. Money, computer, communications and surveillance gear seemed to pass through easier than weaponry. The warrior felt lucky the Beretta and grenades managed to slip through the red-tape tangle. He might have to ask Brognola to pressure the bureaucracy to clear his packages.

That might not be necessary if the recon panned out. Bolan was in Mexico to stop a new wave of terrorist activity directed against citizens from the United States and U.S.-operated businesses. Stony Man suspected a man named Adolfo Valdez was responsible for those acts, and the Executioners knew that the guy possessed the skill, training and combat experience to mastermind commando-style assaults. He was also clearly bitter against the U.S. government and might indeed have the twisted mentality and fanatic hatred to become a terrorist.

Yet Valdez hadn't been difficult to locate. He was in Mexico, using his real name, employed at the Elizondo shop and living in a room of the building. The first forty-eight hours of surveillance hadn't revealed anything to confirm the Farm's suspicions—not until a congregation of midnight visitors arrived for a meeting at the shop.

Three pickup trucks, four cars and two motorcycles had parked by the building. Bolan had counted fourteen men and five women enter the place, and who knew how many more might already be inside. All the visitors were young, most appearing tough and physically fit. The majority wore loose-fitting jackets, and some carried duffel or overnight bags. They could have brought a lot of weapons and explosives for the occasion.

Of course, a group meeting at a garage after hours wasn't proof of a conspiracy, and their bags could be loaded with clothes and camping gear. But the Executioner had no doubt he had found a nest of vipers. He had been a warrior and a manhunter his entire adult life. Bolan's instincts told him the enemy had gathered at the building for more than a social call, but he needed evidence and intended to get it.

The warrior had filmed most of the visitors with a special long-range camera with an infrared lens. The laser microphone would help him get the rest of the proof he needed. He had used numerous types of high-tech surveillance devices in the past. AN/PPS-5 radar gear and AN/TVS-4 night observation devices had been state-of-the-art during the Vietnam conflict. They were primitive compared to the advanced laser technology.

Bolan peered through the Starlight scope to aim the device. The concentrated beam of light found one of several large windows with dark tinted glass. The beam reflected off the pane and bounced back to a receiver unit. It transmitted sound vibrations into a tape recorder. The warrior listened through an earphone and heard voices speaking Spanish. He heard enough to convince him Valdez and company were the terrorists.

Someone mentioned Brian Henderson, the executive from the United States running a branch of a big manufacturing corporation based in Chicago, who along with two junior executives had been brutally murdered in a Mexico City parking lot.

Someone else laughed as he spoke of *"yanqui puto Corey."* That would be Gerald Corey, former U.S. senator, killed while on vacation in Acapulco. They also referred to *"la embajada de los Estados Unidos"*—the United States embassy, Bolan realized. The terrorists also mentioned more names, Anglo and Spanish, which the warrior didn't recognize. He guessed they were probably discussing a hit list of future targets.

"Just give me a little more," Bolan whispered.

The tapes and video footage would be enough to prove Valdez was involved in terrorism. The warrior could simply hand over the data to the Farm's contact and let the Mexican authorities handle it. They could arrest Valdez and any others identified by photos and voiceprints. The Executioner might be able to complete his assignment without having to fire a single shot.

Movement by the side of the building drew Bolan's attention. Three figures approached the hill. Two carried assault rifles held at hip level, muzzles pointed uphill. The third man had a submachine gun, right hand fisted on the pistol grip while the left held a contraption roughly the size and shape of an old-fashioned walkie-talkie.

A tracking device, Bolan guessed, most likely a motion detector or heat sensor. The weapons appeared to be Heckler & Koch G-3 rifles and a H&K MP-5. Serious firepower. All three men moved well in the dark. Quiet and stealthy, they blended into the surrounding shadows as they approached.

The warrior's position was well camouflaged by bushes and shadows from the trees around him, but he knew they would find him. Obviously the men had a general idea of his location. If he grabbed his gear and headed for the other side of the hill, the sudden movement or change of heat patterns would be picked up by the handheld detector. The trio would close in rapidly and spray Bolan's area with full-auto rounds. Even if he survived, the shots would bring out the rest of the terrorists in force.

Better to deal with the three stalkers. The warrior drew his 93-R from the special holster designed to accommodate the silencer attached to the barrel. He moved to the cover of the tree trunk, but left the Marlin where it was. The enemy was coming to him, which left no time to plan much strategy. He would just have to wait and play it by ear.

The first hunter reached the hilltop, rifle held ready. He spotted the mounted laser unit and glanced about for his quarry. The other two arrived moments later. The guy with the detection device consulted it with a frown.

"Where is the bastard?" one of the riflemen rasped in Spanish.

Bolan let them know. Aware he would be discovered at any second, the warrior made the first move. He charged from the tree, Beretta in one fist and combat knife in the other. Bolan snap-aimed the pistol and triggered a 3-round burst as he closed the distance to his opponents. The silenced weapon coughed harshly as the 9 mm slugs slammed into the chest of the man with the detection device. The terrorists with the G-3 weapons presented the greater danger, but the Executioner had to act quickly. There was no time to pick the best target, only to point at upper-torso level and open fire.

His closest opponent turned and tried to swing his rifle toward Bolan, but the warrior was virtually on him before the man could use his weapon. Bolan hammered the metal butt of the knife into the gunman's forearm to prevent his moving the rifle, then slashed the blade in a rising arc and simultaneously aimed the Beretta at the third foe. Sharp steel struck the gunner across the throat as the other man raised his G-3. Bolan squeezed the trigger. Another burst of muted 93-R rounds rasped death. A single rifle shot exploded at the same instant. The unmuffled sound roared and the unshrouded muzzle-flash blazed harsh bright light.

The brief illumination revealed the faces of Bolan's enemies. One displayed a mask of horror and pain, eyes wide and mouth open. Blood poured from the deep cut in his throat, as the man dropped his rifle and grabbed for the terrible wound. The other terrorist's face had been pounded into crimson pulp by the trio of Parabellum rounds.

The faceless man collapsed near the corpse of the terrorist Bolan had shot through the heart. The gunner with the slit throat dropped to his knees and uttered a sickly moan before death claimed him. The shot from his rifle had warned his companions.

Voices shouted from the auto-repair shop. Bolan scooped up one of the H&K rifles as he moved to the edge of the hill. The terrorists swarmed from the building, armed with a variety of weapons. The warrior scanned the scene with the night scope of the laser mike. They numbered about twenty. He wasn't going to waste time taking a head count. Some appeared frightened, a few seemed confused, but the majority wore eager expressions, eyes aglow with excitement. Bolan had seen this expression many times in the past on the faces of terrorists and zealots throughout the world. These were the true devotees of a nameless god of violence and destruction.

The warrior spotted Valdez among the crowd. The terrorist stood taller than most of his followers. His body was strong and lean, built like a middleweight boxer, which in fact, Valdez had been as a youth in San Diego, California. Bolan recognized the man's face from a file photo at Stony Man Farm. His nose was crooked and had been broken on several occasions. His black hair was clipped short, and a trimmed beard concealed a knife scar at the jawline. Bolan knew Valdez bore this mark from a fight with an inmate at San Quentin.

Valdez stared at the hill as if he knew Bolan was watching him. His dark eyes barely blinked, and his mouth formed a firm, determined line. The warrior imagined what thoughts went through Valdez's mind at that moment. Like Bolan, the guy was a former Special Forces NCO and a combat veteran. Valdez would realize the best position for an intruder to spy on the shop would be the hill. He would also know the report of a single rifle shot meant the three-man patrol sent to check the area had been taken out. Yet the fact the place wasn't surrounded by *Federales* or soldiers meant the threat consisted of a small number of opponents, most likely between one and six individuals.

The terrorist boss snapped some curt commands and gestured with the MP-5 subgun in his fist. About a dozen men headed for the hill in a wide horseshoe formation. Others had already advanced in that direction, while a few had made for the vehicles. Valdez and the remaining members of his group took cover by the side of the building, or behind the piles of rubber tires that served as improvised sandbags.

They intended to surround the hill. Valdez assumed that whoever had violated his security would now try to flee as fast as possible. His troops would cover all exits from the hill and the guys in the trucks and cars would speed to the road at the opposite side of the hill to stop anyone attempting to take that route. Valdez's followers acted quickly and obeyed his orders without hesitation. He had clearly drilled his people thoroughly, and they responded well to his command.

Bolan had two options. He could make a run for it and try to break through whatever opposition he encountered, or he could do something Valdez didn't expect. The latter might be more dangerous, yet it would also take the enemy by surprise and show them their leader wasn't infallible. If he could break their confidence in their leader's plan, it might also break their discipline and their willingness to carry out Valdez's orders.

The warrior moved the video camera and tape recorder to the base of a tree to reduce the chance of the evidence being destroyed by a stray bullet. He glanced at the Marlin, about to dismiss it in favor of the confiscated weapons of the slain patrol. An inspired notion changed his mind, and he grabbed the deer gun.

The Executioner moved to a fallen tree near the edge of the hill and assumed a kneeling stance. He deliberately worked the lever to the Marlin, although a round was already in the chamber. The loud click-clack sang into the night as the unused cartridge hopped from the chamber to be replaced by another shell from the tubular magazine. Bolan was certain the enemy heard the sound. He put the walnut buttstock to his shoulder and selected a target among the terrorists on the hill.

He aimed with care. The front sight bisected the upper torso of an ambitious fanatic determined to reach the hilltop. Bolan squeezed the trigger and the Marlin recoiled in his grasp. He watched the terrorist tumble backward downhill, then pumped the lever again, ducking for cover.

A murderous salvo of full-auto fire responded to the single shot from the Marlin. Bullets chewed bits of wood from the log and tore at leaves and branches of surrounding foliage. Bolan stayed down, cradled the Marlin along the crook of an elbow and crawled to the G-3 lying by the laser mike. He crept to the edge and observed the enemy below.

At least four terrorists charged up the hill, guns blazing in the general direction of where Bolan had been when he fired the Marlin. They made no effort to conceal themselves, use available cover or even hunch their backs to present a smaller target. One zealot even whooped some sort of battle cry.

They had obviously heard the metallic click-clack, recognized the sound of a lever-action rifle and decided to rush their unseen enemy before he could get off another shot with the outdated weapon. Bolan's plan had worked better than he expected.

The Heckler & Koch felt more familiar in his hands than the deer gun. Bolan had fired G-3 assault rifles in combat as well as on the range. Seldom had he encountered targets offered so clearly as the four men on the hill. He switched the selector to full-auto and opened fire.

The first burst of 7.62 mm slugs caught a charging gunner in the solar plexus and sternum. The impact hurled him into a sudden back roll down the hill. Another gunman was too busy shooting his M-3 subgun at Bolan's previous position to notice his comrade go down. Bolan fired the G-3 and stitched the terrorist from rib cage to throat.

Startled by the unexpected firepower, the third gunner seemed to freeze in his tracks. Bolan moved him with another trio of H&K missiles. The fourth figure swung his weapon toward the flash of the G-3 muzzle and tried to drop to a knee on the uneven surface. The warrior triggered his rifle and took the hardman down.

As more enemy fire erupted, Bolan scrambled to a new position by a thick tree trunk and a cluster of large rocks. He ejected the spent box magazine from the G-3 and replaced it with a fresh mag filled with twenty rounds. He chambered the first shell as he heard the rumble of an engine amid the howling storm of automatic fire. Two large shapes moved to the road along the base of the hill. A pickup truck and a battered Ford four-door had advanced to try to cut off Bolan's escape or attempt to attack him from a different direction. He followed the vehicles as he plucked an M-26 grenade from his belt. The warrior pulled the pin, popped the spoon and lobbed the grenade as the truck rolled by.

The metal ball landed in the back bed of the vehicle and exploded two seconds later. The fragmentation blast tore the truck apart and ignited the fuel tank. The Ford failed to stop in time and nose-dived into the wreckage as the gas confined in the fuel tank caused a second explosion. The front of the car crumbled and the windshield shattered. A luckless passenger was thrown through jagged remnants of glass to land among the flaming ruins of the truck.

With an angry roar a violent eruption shook the ground under Bolan's feet. He crouched low, but no shrapnel sprayed in his direction. There was another explosion by the rim of the hill. Chunks of earth and an uprooted tree fell downhill.

The enemy was throwing grenades at Bolan's position. He ventured closer on his belly and saw several of the enemy firing weapons while a man swung his arm high. He tossed the grenade, which blew out another section of the hillside. Bolan yanked the pin from an M-26 fragger and pitched it at the enemy clustered below. Terrorists cried out in alarm, and one rose and tried to run. Bolan snap-aimed the G-3 and nailed him with a 3-round volley before he could travel three yards.

The grenade exploded, and at least two bodies were pitched upward by the blast. Bolan had demonstrated it was easier to throw grenades downhill with accuracy than uphill. But his lesson wasn't over yet.

The warrior pulled the pin from another M-26 and hurled the bomb at the garage. The deadly egg landed near the building and rolled to the corner, where it exploded, smashing in the wall and ripping a seam in the foundation. Shrapnel slashed into a terrorist using the building for cover. He stumbled forward, shirt tattered and soaked with blood. The man's face and hands had also been shredded by the blast. More dead than alive, the mangled figure wilted to the ground.

Several terrorists bolted for the vehicles. Bolan guessed they had been rattled by what they had witnessed. Death and destruction appealed to them when they dealt it out to others, but not when they faced being on the receiving end. The terrified fanatics loaded into the cars and trucks as fast as possible, desperate to flee the area.

A head and shoulders rose from a stack of tires. As Bolan recognized Valdez, the man suddenly raised a weapon to his shoulder. It resembled a short shotgun with a huge bore, but the warrior realized Valdez was armed with an M-79 grenade launcher. The terrorist fired the weapon, and a 40 mm explosive shell raced to the hilltop.

The Executioner threw himself to the ground and rolled to shelter by the tree trunk and rock pile. The blast sent a wave of fierce heat sweeping across Bolan, and lumps of earth and loose stones pelted his body with projectile force. The warrior's ears rang and his head throbbed, but he pushed his battered body to a seated position. If he had suffered a concussion, he could lose consciousness unless he kept moving.

Yellow light appeared among the bushes near Bolan, an angry crackle announcing a new threat as he turned to discover flames among the dry foliage. The grenade shell had started the fire, and it had already spread rapidly to a tree. The warrior shook his head to clear it despite the ache. The evidence had to be saved.

The Executioner rose and jogged to the tree where he had placed the camera and recorder. Sore muscles protested, but he kept going. Bolan suddenly realized he had exposed himself to enemy fire, and he had lost the G-3 rifle as well. The explosion had dazed the warrior. He couldn't afford such mistakes. He had to think straight and keep his wits or he'd be dead.

Bolan's hand touched rough bark on the trunk. He knelt by the base of the tree and found the camera and recorder intact. He sighed with relief, but the sensation abruptly vanished as a shriek of agony declared he wasn't alone on the hill.

A figure staggered into view. The man's left hand clutched a burned, bloodied face. His right arm hung limp, attached to the shoulder by some strands of shirt cloth and some shreds of skin. One of Valdez's hardmen had managed to reach the top of the hill only to be victim of his own leader's grenade attack. The wounded man dropped to the ground and fainted as a second figure approached. This terrorist didn't seem to be injured and clutched and M-3 subgun in his fist.

However, the man's attention was fixed on his fallen comrade. He didn't notice Bolan as the warrior drew his Beretta from the shoulder holster. The terrorist slowly turned, saw Bolan and tried to raise his weapon. The Executioner triggered the 93-R and drilled a 9 mm round through the guy's forehead.

The ringing in the warrior's ears began to subside. There were no more shots or explosions. Wary of a trick, Bolan slowly moved to an observation point to examine the scene below. The ground was littered with dead terrorists, and no live opponents were visible. Valdez was gone as well. The terrorist leader had to have fired his M-79 launcher as a parting shot, hoped it would take out Bolan and joined the others in retreat.

The Executioner realized there was no point trying to track the enemy. They knew the area and the roads far better than he did. He needed to get away from the scene of the battle before the police arrived. The auto-repair shop was located in a fairly isolated area, but only thirty kilometers from Mexico City. It was likely that someone heard the sounds of gunshots and explosions, and Bolan didn't plan to be there when the law-and-order troops arrived.

"So much for wrapping up this mission clean and easy," he muttered.

2

"I thought you said you wanted to avoid bloodshed, Señor Belasko?" Miguel Santos commented, addressing Mack Bolan by his cover name.

"Valdez forced me to change my plans."

Santos frowned as he glanced at the screen of a small television set. A news report displayed footage of the ruins at the Elizondo auto-repair shop. Canvas tarps shrouded several bodies while uniformed police kept onlookers at bay. The press had arrived in force and the authorities had their hands full. At least two U.S. television networks were on the scene, reporters and camera crews struggling with local news personnel for better positions.

"They say the body count is at least seventeen," Santos stated. "It may be higher because some of the bodies were torn apart by explosions. Did you have to blow the place up?"

"I did the best I could with the weapons I had. If the rest of my gear had arrived, I would have been able to reduce that shop to a pile of rubble and Valdez wouldn't have gotten away."

Santos's frown pulled his face into an expression of grim disapproval. Stony Man Farm had selected the man to assist Bolan in Mexico, and he was uniquely qualified for the task. Expert in security and surveillance, he had formerly worked for the military and the federal government in Mexico. Santos still had connections with these sources, but ran an independent agency from his office in Mexico City. He handled investigations for industries and occasionally worked on assignment with the *federales* and even the American CIA.

The man spoke fluent English and knew his way around the capital and other cities in central and southern Mexico. Santos had also been born and raised in Chiapas, the impoverished state that spawned the Zapatista peasant revolt, which had first gained international attention in 1994.

"I don't like dealing with guns and explosives, Belasko," Santos began. "You'll have to check with the CIA and whoever else you're associated with to get military weapons. I'm not particularly comfortable with the fact you're carrying that Beretta. This isn't your American Wild West. People go to prison in Mexico just for having a single round of 9 mm or .45-caliber ammunition in their possession."

"Yeah," Bolan replied, "but when the people you're up against start to shoot at you, it's nice to have a gun to shoot back."

"I did manage to get that rifle for you."

"The Marlin? Thanks, but I think I'll try to get something else for the next time."

"I don't understand why you went to the Elizondo shop alone last night," Santos remarked. "Of course we were conducting surveillance on the area, but when you saw a large group had gathered for a suspicious meeting, you should have contacted us. The situation was too dangerous for you to handle on your own.''

''That would have put your life in jeopardy,'' the warrior insisted. ''No offense, but you're not a combat soldier. Better to handle a firefight by myself than have untrained and inexperienced backup.''

Santos sighed. ''What's done is done. At least you managed to come back unharmed, and you certainly proved Valdez is involved with the terrorists. That was the reason for your visit to my country.''

''Part of it,'' Bolan acknowledged.

The warrior had confirmed Valdez was involved in the terrorist conspiracy, yet Bolan was a soldier, not an investigator. Recon might be part of his job, but his mission wouldn't be finished until the enemy had been put out of action—one way or another.

A key turned in the lock to the office door. Bolan instinctively moved his hand to his open windbreaker, near the Beretta holstered under his arm. The door opened and Ellena Santos entered the office. She was an attractive woman, a few years younger than her brother Miguel, and assisted his security investigations. She smiled at Bolan, her large dark eyes meeting his gaze for a moment.

''Have you two been watching the news?'' she inquired.

''We've seen it,'' Santos assured her. ''It's the top story. What can you add to it?''

Ellena perched on the corner of the desk, opened her purse and removed a small notepad.

"You made quite a mess at the auto shop, Mike," she told Bolan, using the first name of his cover identity of Mike Belasko. "The police haven't been able to identify most of the dead left at the site. Four were ex-convicts, identified by fingerprints. They all had criminal records for violence and all originally came from Chiapas state. Valdez would have been easily identified, but his body was not found.

"Yeah. I knew he got away."

"Perhaps he was wounded during the battle," Santos suggested. "Maybe his body will be found in a few days, dead from injuries by stray bullets or flying shrapnel."

"I wouldn't count on that," Bolan advised. "They probably have some wounded survivors, but they obviously won't take them to a hospital. The terrorists may need medicine or supplies. Any reports of medical items stolen from a clinic or pharmacy might give us some idea which direction they headed."

"We already know most of the Zapatista bases are in the Lancondon jungle in Chiapas," Santos remarked. "The army didn't have any luck trying to find the rebels in the past. That's probably where Valdez and his people are now."

"Valdez won't be easy to find anymore," Ellena agreed. "When he thought he could safely use his real name and openly work and live in Mexico City, it was easy to keep track of him. Too bad we couldn't have had him arrested then. It might take a long time to find him now that he'll be hiding from the authorities.''

''Maybe he won't want to hide for long,'' Bolan stated. ''Have you listened to the tapes? I couldn't understand a lot of what was said.''

''The terrorists spoke in detail about the assassinations they committed and plans for other crimes of murder and sabotage they hope to carry out in the future. I got legal authorization from a federal judge to conduct surveillance on Valdez and the auto-repair shop, so the tapes and video footage would be valid evidence in court. Naturally I didn't mention your role in this business. I'm not so sure the judge would have approved of that.''

Ellena crossed her legs. She smiled at Bolan, aware his eyes were drawn to her although he tried to keep his gaze at face level. Bolan turned to Santos and hoped the guy hadn't noticed his appreciation of Ellena's beauty. Mexican men tended to be protective of their sisters.

''Do you have any idea what we should do now?'' Santos inquired. ''I suppose we could turn the whole matter over to the *federales* and the military. They may not be able to do any more than we could, but at least they'd know about Valdez and they'll be no worse off than they were before.''

''Give them the information about Valdez,'' Bolan replied. ''We're not in competition with the federal authorities. If they can find Valdez and put him out of business, that's fine with me. But I don't think Valdez will stay in hiding for long. He might have recruited his troops from the ranks of the Zapatistas, but they're not really concerned with the impoverished conditions or hardships of the Indians in Chiapas state. They're violent fanatics. I recognize the species. Seen the type enough times in the past to know that's what we're dealing with. They follow Valdez because he leads them down the path of destruction and carnage.''

"He led at least seventeen of them to the slaughter when you hit the shop last night," Ellena remarked.

"That's why Valdez will have to retaliate soon," Bolan replied. "He lost face when he had to retreat. If he wants those mad dogs to continue to believe in him, he'll have to show them he can still lead them to victory."

"So he'll launch another attack?" Santos asked.

Bolan nodded. "We just have to be ready when he does it."

3

The harsh drone of a buzzer alerted Hal Brognola. Someone was trying to contact him. He glanced at the control panel and saw the flashing red light on a button bearing the emblem of an eagle surrounded by a circle of small stars. The big Fed pressed the button, and a large section of a wall in the War Room slid back to display a monitor screen.

Brognola punched in an access code to acknowledge the message had been received, and the President of the United States appeared on the monitor. He sat at a small metal desk, computer keyboard in front of him. The Commander in Chief wore a sweatshirt, a towel draped over his shoulders and a baseball cap perched on his head. The President had apparently been jogging when Brognola first tried to contact him. He wasted no time responding to the Stony Man call when he returned to the White House.

"I was hoping I'd hear from you," the Man said, his voice a bit raspier than usual. "Wondered if I'd have to count on CNN to let me know what you people have been up to."

"That business in Mexico wasn't pretty," Brognola replied, "but at least it was only the bad guys on the receiving end this time. My man in the field confirmed our suspicions about Mr. Valdez. He's all we thought him to be and more."

"Is he still alive?"

Brognola wasn't sure if he meant Valdez or Bolan.

"Yeah. Both of them are. Striker's a little frustrated that his quarry got away, but Valdez is probably having fits after what happened. He's dropped out of sight, but Striker doesn't figure that'll last long."

"Does he know where Valdez is?"

"No, but he thinks Valdez will try another hit soon and has a couple ideas what the next target will be. Valdez needs to restore the confidence of his troops. That means he'll go for something big."

The President frowned. "I don't like the sound of that, Hal."

"If he tries a big target, he puts himself at big risk, and that means we'll have a greater chance to catch him."

"And he'll have a chance to cause greater damage and kill more people."

"Valdez is going to do what he's going to do, Mr. President. We can't change his choice. We can just try to be ready to deal with him when he makes his move."

"You say your man thinks he knows what the target will be?"

"Well, he used a laser microphone eavesdropping device to record a conversation Valdez had with his terrorist cronies. They bragged about killing Henderson and Corey. They also discussed some possible future targets. Some of these were individuals marked for assassination—American businessmen, some Mexican nationals regarded as Yankee sympathizers and thus traitors to Valdez's way of thinking.''

"We think he betrayed the United States of America and he thinks the United States betrayed him and Latin Americans in general," the President remarked. "Right now, I don't really care why he's involved in terrorism. I just want him stopped."

"That's the idea. Striker doesn't think Valdez will go after any of these individuals next. Killing them would be small accomplishments. He'll want something that will rock us on our heels and make headlines around the world. Striker thinks that narrows it down to two potential choices from those discussed by the terrorists. One is a large automobile-assembly factory in northern Mexico, owned by one of the major U.S. car manufacturers.''

"The one that shut down plants in Michigan in the 1980s and put a lot of people out of work before setting up operations south of the border?"

"That's the one," Brognola confirmed. "The other target would be the U.S. embassy in Mexico City. Since the enemy is based in the southern part of Mexico and previous attacks have been in the south and central areas, including Mexico City, Striker figures the terrorists have better Intelligence sources, more manpower and easier access to weapons and supplies in this area. It would also be easier to do a hit-and-run attack in a place they're familiar with that's close to home base so they can head for the shelter of their jungle hideaway. Since Valdez needs to act soon to restore the faith in his followers, the embassy seems the more likely target.''

"Unless Valdez suspects we know about his plans and decides to change them.''

"The terrorists at the auto-repair shop knew somebody was watching them from a hilltop. That's when they went after Striker and the gunfight occurred. Valdez didn't know about the laser microphone and probably won't guess we know what they were talking about.''

"All right," the President began. "I don't like the idea of our embassy being used as bait. I want everything humanly possible done to protect the embassy and the lives of the people who work there and innocent bystanders in the area.''

"We'll do everything we can. When you're dealing with terrorists there's no way to make sure anyone is really safe. Striker is the best. Nobody could handle this assignment better.''

"I know. Good luck and keep in touch, Hal.''

The President hit the keyboard and the monitor went blank.

ADOLFO VALDEZ STARED at the photographs mounted on corkboard. His agents in Mexico City had been gathering intelligence about the target for almost a month. They had taken pictures from different directions, covering every side of the building. Every door and window was marked. The site had been observed twenty-four hours a day. Notes provided information about embassy security, estimated number of personnel on hand and the daily schedules of the ambassador and other key diplomats stationed there.

He had wanted more time to plan the attack. Valdez appreciated the great risk involved. Striking out at a target in the middle of the capital city was dangerous. Security at the embassy itself wasn't a major problem. He respected the ability of the Marines assigned to the site, but they were few in number and served a largely ceremonial role that prevented them from being heavily armed. They might have access to more firepower, but Valdez planned a hit-and-run assault that would last only scant minutes. The Marines would still be getting weapons from the arms room while the terrorists made their escape.

The police and *federales* presented a greater problem. They would swarm to the site as fast as possible with every available man and vehicle. Getting out of the city would be a major accomplishment and the military would probably be called in to set up roadblocks and search parties as well. Even if he had months to plan the attack it wouldn't be easy.

He didn't have the luxury of time. The incident at the auto-repair shop demanded Valdez take action rapidly or lose the respect of his followers. Most had been reluctant to accept a stranger born in the United States. They immediately recognized him as an outsider despite his name, physical appearance and fluency in Spanish. Actually he discovered some of the words and expressions commonly used among Hispanics in southern California were different from those spoken in southern Mexico. A slight accent could be detected at times.

He had to prove he was a better leader because he came from the United States. He knew the Americans. Anglos might visit Mexico because "Latin charm" appealed to them, but they tended to grow tired of the culture and yearn for more familiar settings. They would congregate with other English-speaking visitors, in places that featured food that suited their taste and music they recognized.

Valdez also knew what sort of security methods were most likely to be adopted by U.S. companies operating in Mexico. They had set up business south of the border because they wanted a cheap labor force. They tended to regard their workers as ignorant, slow-witted, lazy and untrustworthy. They considered Mexicans in general to be dirty little thieves. Corporate security was usually more concerned with catching employees stealing from offices and assembly line than with protecting the company from an outside threat.

Most of all, Valdez's background in the U.S. Army and Special Forces convinced the others he was fit to lead them. His skill with weapons, ability in strategy and tactics, and courage in participating in the attacks himself truly impressed the rebels. Zapata and Villa had been battlefield commanders. Valdez knew he had to emulate that style if he expected the others to believe in him.

Of course, he was also able to supply them with better arms and equipment due to his connections with illegal gunrunners. This had probably been the reason they first allowed him to put his foot through the figurative door, yet superior weapons and gear meant nothing without the ability to use them.

Exceptional skill, Valdez thought as his mind moved to the one-sided battle at the auto-repair shop. The enemy on the hill had certainly possessed extraordinary combat ability. Whoever they were, they had the advantage of higher ground, but that shouldn't have been enough to allow them to hold off the charge by Valdez's people. Judging by the gunfire and grenades used by the enemy, Valdez guessed there couldn't have been more than three or four men on that hilltop.

He had seen only one for an instant during the battle. The silhouette of the man's figure appeared for a fragment of a second, set against the fiery light of burning foliage. The man was tall, lean and moved like an Olympic athlete. Valdez had tried to raise his MP-5 to fire on the figure, but the target was gone in the blink of an eye. Besides, the enemy was out of range for Valdez's H&K submachine gun. There was no time to get a rifle to try to pick the man off or to lob more M-79 grenade shells in hope of taking him out. Valdez had already ordered a retreat. His people were being cut to pieces, and the military or police would soon be headed for the site.

One man, Valdez thought. Could one man have done that to his forces?

He heard the canvas flap stir and turned to the entrance to his tent. Hector Arguello stood at the threshold. At forty-one, Arguello was the "old man" in Valdez's outfit. Small and balding, with a soft round face and a neatly trimmed mustache speckled with gray, he seemed out of place in the rebel camp. A gray suit and striped tie would have appeared more natural to the man than an over-size set of jungle fatigues, battered old boots and .45 pistol on his hip.

Yet Arguello was a veteran of the 23rd September Movement. During the 1970s and early 1980s, the left-wing terrorist group had been the largest and most feared in Mexico. Many members had been arrested or killed, but Arguello had survived. Valdez had been reluctant to work with the man because Arguello had formerly been a Communist. However, Arguello no longer endorsed communism, and condemned Karl Marx as "another white European with a plan to exploit the working masses." His experience made him a valuable supporter and adviser to Valdez. The fact he had survived several encounters with the police and *federales* and managed to avoid arrest for almost two decades, earned Arguello's respect among the others as well.

"Still plan to attack the gringo embassy?" Arguello asked.

He glanced at the corkboard and a street map of Mexico City sprawled across Valdez's small field desk, pinned down by the MP-5 subgun. He knew the answer before Valdez spoke.

"We have to do it," the terrorist leader declared.

"We have to do something. You know how dangerous this is, Adolfo."

"No more dangerous than the bank robberies carried out by the 23rd September Movement in Mexico City. You faced basically the same problems we have now."

"And not all of us got away when we robbed those banks. We lost quite a few comrades. Some were arrested and some were killed."

"We can do it, Hector. I know we can."

"Those robberies were twenty years ago. Things are different now. The police and federal agents have more helicopters. They can move faster and they work together better than they used to. They have infrared searchlights on those helicopters too, so they can track better at night."

"I don't plan to do it at night," Valdez explained. "Best time will be in the day. I've studied the ambassador's schedule and how the Marines handle watch duties. The best time for the strike will be 1300 hours approximately. That's when the ambassador leaves in his limousine. We're going to kill that bastard and cause as much destruction to the embassy building as possible."

Arguello approached the board. His expression remained grim as he scanned the photographs and observation notes. Valdez moved to his cot. His belongings were few. Virtually everything he owned was stuffed in a duffel bag by the foot of the cot. He fished a pack of cigarettes from the bag and glanced about the tent. It was roughly the same size as the prison cell in San Quentin, he realized. For a while, this would be his home.

"Before we start carrying out these ambitions," Arguello began, "you'd better take care of a problem right here in the camp."

"What problem?"

"García claims you've proved to be a failure. He says you're not fit to lead us. I think he might intend to kill you, Adolfo."

"And what do you think of that, Hector?"

"I don't think García is fit to lead a street gang in a liquor store holdup, but you have to deal with this."

Valdez frowned. "Do you think he'll listen to reason?"

"García is not a very reasonable man," Arguello replied. "He has drawn others to join our little army because he is a fiery, emotional speaker. Like you, García is a fighting man with deep feelings of anger and resentment toward the government of this country and the Americans. Unfortunately he also resents you. García would probably be leading these people if you were not here."

"But you said he's not fit to lead."

"García is a bull too eager to charge the cape without thinking. Yet he is respected by many of the young men here. They're filled with machismo and always ready to fight. García would get them killed."

"What about you?"

"He wouldn't get me killed. I'll leave if García takes command. Eventually I'll find another revolutionary group. Don't expect me to get involved by openly taking your side against García. This is between you and him, Adolfo. I'm just letting you know the situation."

"Thanks," Valdez said with a sigh.

He dropped the cigarette to the dirt floor and crushed it underfoot. Valdez considered taking the MP-5, but decided against it. He didn't want to appear fearful or distrustful of his own followers. He couldn't lead them without their trust and confidence, so he had to present the impression the feeling was mutual. Besides, García wouldn't lie in wait to kill him by ambush. That wasn't the man's style.

Or so Valdez hoped. If he was wrong, staying inside the tent would be as dangerous as venturing outside to confront García. People tended to commit murder without witnesses, so it might be wise to move into view of the others.

Arguello took a seat on the cot. He had warned Valdez, and that was all the help he would give. *"Buena suerte,"* Arguello said.

Good luck. Valdez's luck seemed to have taken a nosedive. He couldn't dwell on what had happened. Valdez told himself luck was an illusion. He would keep control of the rebels and lead them to new victories. García wasn't going to stop him. Valdez would do whatever necessary to see to that.

He emerged from the tent. The camp was unusually quiet. More than fifty people were stationed at the covert site, yet Valdez heard no conversations, singing, laughter or shouts of anger. No one was within four yards of his tent. Few lingered by the nearest tents, and none stood at the clearing in the center of the camp. They didn't look directly at him. Valdez noticed everyone wore full uniforms, with shirts, boots and headgear. Most tended to adopt more relaxed attire at the camp, favoring sandals or bare feet to boots, only an undershirt or no shirt, perhaps cutoff shorts.

No one was relaxed now. Most carried weapons, with spare ammo pouches on their belt gear. They knew a confrontation would occur within the camp, and they were ready in case all hell broke loose. Valdez wondered if they had already picked which side they would fight for. Would most back Valdez, or had García managed to convince the majority to support his bid for power? Probably they'd accept whoever came out ahead.

He glanced about the camp. Rows of canvas tents, three outhouse-style latrines and the improvised "parade field" in the center comprised the bivouac area. The latter was simply a clearing worn flat by activity. No vehicles were present. Nothing with wheels could travel to the site, hidden in the thicket of bush, ferns, tangled vines and towering trees. A natural ceiling of tree branches provided constant shade and helped conceal the base from observation by planes or helicopters. Camouflage netting also draped the tents to contribute to their invisibility from above.

"You looking for something, Chief?" a baritone voice inquired.

The question was asked in a tone that demanded a reply. Valdez recognized the voice and turned to see García approach. A big man, García stood an inch taller than Valdez and weighed about thirty pounds more. His burly chest, wide shoulders and thickly muscled arms could intimidate any rational man. The hostile expression on García's broad face proved even more threatening. His lips twisted into a scowl, and his eyes glared with rage.

Two of García's closest friends accompanied the big man. Juan and Pedro often trailed dutifully behind García, content to be lesser beings in the orbit of their hero. Physical opposites, the pair would have seemed comical without García. Juan was stick thin and looked almost frail. A long neck emphasized his bobbing Adam's apple, and sad eyes and large ears added to his odd appearance. Pedro was shorter, with a wide, bulging belly and stocky limbs. His moon face and double chin contributed to a buffoon image.

Valdez guessed the two had experienced a lot of grief and ridicule before they became García's toadies. Nobody was apt to laugh at them when they stood beside the fierce brute. Valdez noticed García was unarmed, but his amigos carried holstered pistols and machetes in their belts. They hadn't been clearing the brush around the camp, so the big jungle knives weren't a good sign for Valdez.

"Maybe you're looking for someplace to hide," García remarked. "Never know when you might have to run away again."

"A coward runs away," Valdez replied. "But a wise man doesn't get himself and his friends killed because he doesn't retreat when that's the sane choice to make. If you have something to say, just say it, García."

"I say you got a lot of our people killed the other night. Everybody thought you were so smart. So sure of yourself you even used your real name and worked outside Mexico City to be close enough to gather information. How do you like this stinking hole compared to your nice big apartment in the city?"

"I've been in worse places," Valdez said. "I should have come here before, but I didn't think the American or Mexican authorities would suspect me. I thought it safe to use my real name. In fact, I had worried that trying to assume a false identity might be more risky because I came here using a real passport."

"You were wrong, Valdez. That mistake cost a lot of lives of my people. *My* people! Not yours. I am an Indian from Chiapas. You are just an American with a Spanish name."

"I am Mexican. My family came from this country. A Mexican is still a Mexican. Perhaps more so when forced to live among Anglos."

"We've all heard your sad story of how the white gringos lied and manipulated you into joining their Army," García said with a sneer. "Then you saw how they regard Latinos when they invaded Panama. You went to prison because you protested the bigotry of the U.S. government and then vowed to do everything possible to help us gain independence. So noble. So stupid! How can you understand what we're fighting for? You've never had the Feds drive you from your home because a lumber company wanted your land.

You haven't seen family members die because the government fails to give us adequate medical care.''

"And you've never led your people in a successful mission against enemy targets," Valdez declared. "You choose to dismiss our previous victories, but you never came close to anything like them before I joined this group. We did lose some good brothers and sisters the other night. We also knew all of us wouldn't survive this war. Many Zapatistas died in battle against the soldiers before, and more will die before this is over.''

"And maybe you should be the next to go."

García gestured with a massive hand and pointed at the ground between himself and Valdez. Juan and Pedro stepped forward and drew their machetes. Valdez shuffled back and glared at the pair. They smiled in unison and suddenly jammed the blades of the jungle knives into the earth. One handle pointed toward Valdez, the other toward García.

"You talk too much, gringo," García announced. "We'll settle this the way men with real balls deal with a problem. We find out who the better man is. The winner leads and the loser dies."

Valdez glanced at the machetes. Juan and Pedro moved aside. They joined a ring of spectators who surrounded the parade field. The entire population of the camp formed a circle to watch the confrontation between their leader and his burly challenger.

"This is a stupid way to choose a leader," Valdez stated. "A man's mind is more important than his muscles. A leader must be able to think, plan and organize. Which of us is better at personal combat is a moot point and proves nothing.''

"It proves you'll die a coward!" García snarled.

He suddenly lunged for the nearer machete and reached down to grab the handle. Valdez closed in swiftly and swung a boot. The heel smashed into García's mouth as he seized the jungle knife. The kick snapped the big man's head back and sent him tumbling to the ground, but he held on to the machete. Steel flashed as the long blade was yanked free of the ground.

Valdez quickly grabbed the other knife and pulled it from the earth. García rose, blood streaming from his mouth. His upper lip had been split by the kick and a front tooth was broken, but the pain only fueled his fury. García slashed his machete in a vicious cross-body sweep. Valdez met the attack with his weapon. Blades clashed with a metallic ring. Valdez's left arm swung a short, fast hook and punched his adversary in the side of the jaw.

The big man staggered from the blow, then charged with a wild overhead swing. García's blade might have cut Valdez in two, but the other man dodged the furious attack. The brute's anger had made him careless and out of control. Valdez saw a clear target and attacked.

His machete slashed into García's wrist above the weapon in his fist. Sharp steel cut muscle and bone. García screamed and dropped his knife. His severed hand fell beside it as blood spouted from the stump of his maimed wrist. Valdez's left fist scored another hook to the jaw and drove García to his knees.

"Goodbye, you son of a bitch," Valdez rasped as he raised his machete.

He delivered the final stroke, and the crowd gasped. Valdez thought he heard Juan and Pedro cry out "No" as the heavy blade chopped through García's neck. Silence followed the decapitation. Valdez's heart beat fast and hard, the pulse behind his ear sounded like a drum, yet he detected the liquid gurgle as blood pumped from García's neck.

He looked away from the headless corpse. Valdez felt his stomach turn, but the faces of the spectators suddenly eased his illness. They were awestruck, stunned and impressed by the outcome of the duel. The terrorists admired strength and lethal skill. Valdez knew they would follow him without question, convinced the victory in this trial by combat meant fate had chosen him to lead them.

Valdez pointed his machete at Juan and Pedro. The pair appeared to be in a state of shock, horrified by the death of their hero and terrified to see García's blood still on the blade.

"You two," Valdez declared. "Bury him. Make it quick. We have work to do."

4

The monolith appeared mounted on a foundation of bricks and glass. The four sides to the structure displayed a colorful collage of designs, figures, emblems and letters. Different styles of art reflected Mexico past and present. Aztec warriors stood beside modern Olympic athletes, marked by the symbol of five interlocking circles. Mayan gods and calendar figures surrounded a stone banner that bore the legend Universidad Nacional de Méjico.

Rectangular windows positioned along the walls seemed to blend into the network of designs and elaborate patterns. One might easily have mistaken the building for a great monument if one failed to notice the windows, or the antennae on the roof of the structure.

Karl Brunjes noticed the site had caught the attention of his companion. "Pretty fancy, isn't it?" he remarked to Mack Bolan. "That's the Central Library of the National University of Mexico."

"You have to return some books, Karl?" Bolan asked.

Brunjes shrugged, aware his companion hadn't met him to discuss local architecture. The Company man was a cerebral sort, a scholar well versed in history and culture. He liked to talk about these subjects whenever possible and enjoyed playing tour guide.

Nearly as tall as Bolan, Brunjes was big-boned and husky. He had been a top football player in college and held a 1st dan black belt in kano judo. However, a traffic accident had broken both legs and smashed a hip. Brunjes walked with a limp, and the steel pins in his hip obviously caused pain on occasion. The injuries meant he would probably spend most of his CIA career behind a desk.

Although Brunjes spoke fluent Spanish, his appearance immediately labeled him an Anglo. Light skinned, with tawny hair, the guy wouldn't make a very convincing Mexican. Bolan noticed Brunjes wore his hair a bit longer than most CIA personnel. He hoped that meant a streak of maverick remained. The Executioner didn't trust anyone who was so blindly loyal to the Company he could no longer think for himself.

They walked to a parking lot. Brunjes handed Bolan a set of keys and tilted his head toward a gray van. The warrior unlocked the driver's-side door and climbed inside. He opened the passenger side for Brunjes while he inspected the vehicle.

"We did the best we could on short notice," the CIA officer explained. "The van is armor-plated with a titanium alloy. Very strong and hard, but lightweight in case you need speed in an emergency. Got a hell of an engine under the hood. May not look like much, but this is a tough street machine. Almost like driving a small tank.''

Bolan had driven a few tanks. The van didn't remind him much of them, but it was vaguely similar to some specialized vehicles he'd used in the past. It couldn't compare with war wagons he had employed against the Mob in earlier days, but the rig was still a well-made machine with admirable modifications for Bolan's work.

''The windows are made of bulletproof glass,'' Brunjes continued. ''Those brackets under the dash are for a CB radio and police scanner.''

''I've got communications gear that's a little more sophisticated than that,'' Bolan remarked. ''At least I have some of it. Did the rest arrive at the embassy?''

''A couple more pouches came in. I put them in the back. Take a look.''

Bolan slipped between the seat backs into the back of the rig and saw three large aluminum cases. He unlatched the first and opened it to find an advanced transceiver computer. Designed to transmit radio messages as well as receive, the device could also detect most frequencies that escaped conventional radio equipment. It was equipped with an audiorecorder and translating capability with a 200,000-word memory in seven languages.

Another case contained a laser microphone unit to replace the one damaged during the auto-repair shop gun battle. The last case held a large steel pistol with a holster, spare magazines, three boxes of shells and a cleaning kit. Bolan removed the handgun and pulled back the slide to check the chamber. Brunjes looked at the long thick barrel, heavy frame and big grips.

"That thing looks even nastier than that Beretta you've got," he remarked. "What the hell is it?"

"A .44 Magnum Desert Eagle," Bolan answered.

"Uh-huh," the CIA man replied. "So now you're packing the most powerful pistol in the world?"

"There are three or four handguns more powerful, including the .50 Magnum Desert Eagle. You can stop a Cape buffalo with a single round using one of those handheld cannons, but the size of the cartridges and the necessary size of the weapon means you have limited ammunition capacity and a bulky pistol. The .44 Magnum is the most powerful handgun that's practical for combat."

"Great. But isn't one big, bad pistol enough?"

"Depends on what you're up against," Bolan replied. "What happened to the rest?"

"You're lucky we got the pistols through diplomatic channels. They're getting fastidious about what's transported in those pouches. You know there have been some incidents of smuggling and gunrunning through diplomatic pouches."

"Yeah," Bolan replied, "so I've heard. The Company was supposed to have cleared our deliveries, which included weapons and explosives."

"You've got the pistols and some grenades."

"Not enough. I should have received an M-16 assault rifle with a Starlight scope, M-203 grenade launcher attachment and armor-piercing 5.56 mm ammo and 40 mm grenade cartridges.''

"Even CIA has a problem trying to justify transporting that sort of hardware to an embassy on foreign soil.''

"Excuses aren't much help. If I'd had that M-16 and the launcher the other night, this Valdez business would be over and I'd be out of your face.''

"Well, you sure managed to kill a lot of people without the assault rifle and a grenade launcher.''

"But Valdez got away.''

"Even so, do you really think you need a grenade launcher?''

"Valdez had one. I was lucky he didn't waste me, Karl. We can't count on luck, and I can't do my job unless I have all the tools I need—including the hardware that makes you uncomfortable.''

"It would make any reasonable man uncomfortable,'' Brunjes insisted. "Armor-piercing bullets aren't even used by the military except in extreme combat situations.''

"You should have seen how extreme that situation was on that hill. We're dealing with an enemy who doesn't care about the rules. They'll hit us with everything they've got, and we'd better be ready when they do.''

Brunjes sighed and shook his head. "And you think they'll attack the U.S. embassy next?''

"Yeah. And I don't think we'll have to wait long for it to happen,'' Bolan replied. "Valdez has to prove he's an old-fashioned Zapata-Villa type commander. He can't do that if he's hiding from us."

"So you've said before. We've made changes in security according to your theory. Personally I don't think it's enough. If we're really going to protect the embassy, we ought to call in the Mexican army and have the place surrounded by armed troops and tanks."

"That might be a deterrent," the warrior told him. "Valdez might decide to go after another target if he sees that kind of opposition. Just as likely he'll use a different style of attack. He could still shell the embassy with rocket launchers or mortar rounds from half a mile away."

"Holy shit," Brunjes rasped. "You really think he'd go to such extremes? He could slaughter hundreds of people if he did something like that."

"Valdez doesn't care about that. He and the other terrorists regard the Mexican military to be the enemy as well as the U.S. government. They wouldn't object to killing a bunch of soldiers who got in the way of their plan."

"How do we know they won't shell the place even if there aren't any troops around the embassy?"

"That's unlikely because they wouldn't want to use long-range heavy artillery unless necessary. Valdez may have some impressive supply lines due to his arms-dealer days, but access to mortars, rockets and other devices would be limited. They won't want to use up what they've got. Besides, Valdez isn't a mad dog.

He won't risk the lives of any more innocent bystanders than necessary."

"Or so we can hope," Brunjes remarked. "I've always heard terrorists don't care about innocent lives. They even want high civilian body counts in order to create greater fear and terror."

"Terrorists aren't all alike. They're ruthless and extremists, but some still care about human life—to some degree at least, if only to maintain sympathy for their cause with the public. Valdez is a disillusioned patriot. I've studied the man's file. He's not the type to resort to wanton destruction just for the sake of destruction. The same may not be true about everybody in his group."

"Okay. You're running this show. We'll do this your way, Belasko. I still don't see that you need an assault rifle with a grenade launcher and armor-piercing bullets to take on these guys in a gun battle within the city limits."

"That'll depend on what they're using against us," Bolan replied. "No point debating this issue with you, Karl. The M-16 and other gear didn't arrive, and it's not your fault it didn't get here. I'll just have to improvise with what's available and hope it will be enough."

"What if it isn't?"

"It'll have to be. What about the security for the embassy."

"We're following your advice. The Marines have been warned there's a possibility the place might be targeted by the same terrorists who took out Gerald

Corey. He was a political figure, so they'll take this warning seriously. All the cameras and monitors are being checked daily to be sure everything is in top working order. Good thing. Turned out two cameras had flawed lenses and registered blurred images on the screen. One video recorder had to be replaced because it had been recording nothing but static images due to a worn-out part. Two others needed new tapes.

"The tapes are being changed every day now and we're keeping them on file," the CIA man went on. "Sometimes old tapes were being recorded over. That won't happen now. The number of Marines on duty will appear to be the same to anyone outside the building, but inside the embassy more men are on standby in case of an emergency. The unit commander has doubled the troops on duty at night because he figures that's when the place is most likely to be attacked."

"Tell him not to make that assumption," Bolan said. "A few years ago some Navy SEALs were assigned to test security at U.S. military bases. They discovered some installations were secured tight as a drum after dark, but they could stroll right on base during the day. Make sure the troops are alert to danger twenty-four hours. Nobody can afford to drop his guard until this is over."

Brunjes nodded.

"Okay. How prepared are the Marines? Are they armed?"

"Their weapons are kept in an arms room. That's standard operating procedure as I understand."

"That's SOP, and it's dangerous in a situation like this. I know how they usually work guard duty in the military. Weapons are secured until issued for a man's watch. As often as not ammunition isn't even given to anyone except the officer or NCO in charge—and that's probably just a magazine loaded with shells for the pistol he'll carry during the watch. If the grunts on guard duty are issued ammunition, they're generally ordered to keep the loaded magazine in an ammo pouch and not to load the weapon unless ordered to do so or circumstances make this the logical choice of action."

"But that's a safety precaution to prevent accidents with a loaded firearm."

"Do you recall what happened in Lebanon on April 18, 1983?" Bolan asked.

"The terrorist car-bomb attack in Beirut," Brunjes answered. "A suicide driver hit the Marine barracks with a load of explosive and killed more than two hundred Marines."

"Two hundred and forty-one. That vehicle drove past several Marines who couldn't do a damn thing to stop it because they carried unloaded weapons. By the time they got the magazines out of the pouches and into their rifles it was too late. A few days later, another suicide driver tried the same stunt on a British base in Beirut. Some SAS commandos shot and killed the driver before he could reach his target."

"Jesus," the CIA man groaned. "The diplomats will have a fit if the marines are running around the embassy with loaded guns. They'll never agree to that, Belasko.''

"Then at least have the weapons out of the arms room, issued to troops and secured in wall lockers or weapons racks somewhere close enough to be reached in a crisis. Store the ammo separate from the weapons. Those Marines have been trained to use firearms properly. If you can't trust a man with a gun, you shouldn't issue him one—with or without ammunition. Put the guy in the motor pool or on KP duty, but you don't give him a gun.''

"I'll talk to the commander. We'll do the best we can.''

"The ambassador is a likely target for assassination. What's being done to increase his safety?''

"Some work was done on his limo. Armor plating similar to what was used on this van. He's not happy about it, but I got him to agree to wear a Kevlar vest whenever he sets foot outside the embassy. He's also being accompanied by at least two bodyguards instead of the usual aides. Whenever possible I'm going with him myself.''

"You're not wearing a vest now," Bolan observed. "What sort of heat are you packing?''

"You mean now?" Brunjes asked with surprise. "I'm not carrying a gun. Didn't think I'd need one.''

"What do you carry when you think you might need one?''

"Snub-nose .38 Smith & Wesson.''

"That's okay for a backup piece, but you need something with more stopping power, greater range and accuracy. A 9 mm or larger caliber with a barrel no less than four inches. You're big enough you shouldn't have any trouble handling a .357 Magnum or a .45 auto."

"I've fired some guns like that on the range," Brunjes said. "I'm just not used to carrying a gun that size."

"Try to get used to it and make sure you carry it all the time. We don't know what Valdez might decide to do. He might scrap plans to attack the embassy itself and go after some diplomats for individual strikes on the street. That could make you a target if you're spotted leaving the embassy. If he suspects you might be CIA instead of a diplomat, that'll just increase the odds he'll want you dead."

"That's a comforting thought," Brunjes remarked. "Are you always so cheerful?"

"I'd be in a better mood if all my gear had arrived, but that's not your fault, Karl. What about civilian employees inside the embassy? Valdez could have a spy planted among the Mexican nationals working as servants or kitchen personnel."

"We don't have very many civilian employees, and none has been hired since Valdez arrived in Mexico. Not very likely we've got a terrorist inside the embassy."

"No," Bolan agreed, "but you could have a potential informer. Someone who might be willing to give Valdez information for money or because he secretly hates gringos. Just try to keep the staff from knowing any details. That goes for the Americans as well as the

Mexican nationals. Some people will sell out their country for thirty pieces of silver, and some just can't keep their mouths shut if they've had a few drinks with a *señorita*. Most of Valdez's followers are men, but he has a few females in his outfit as well.''

"Hell. You sure we can trust each other? How about Santos and his sister? No doubts about them?''

"So far so good," Bolan answered. "They'll help me handle the surveillance outside the embassy and serve as the liaison with the police. If it hits the fan, we want to have the cops set up roadblocks pronto and clear the area of innocent bystanders. I'm more concerned with them taking care of those functions than backing us up in a firefight. Then they can arrest whatever is left of Valdez's attack force.''

"How bad do you think it's going to be?'' Brunjes asked.

"I don't know. Just prepare for the worst and that way we won't be disappointed.''

5

Mexico City is one of the most heavily populated areas in the world. Like all modern cities, the capital of Mexico swarmed with taxicabs, buses and delivery vehicles of all sizes. Cars and pickup trucks competed for space, and the right-of-way seemed to go to whoever could bully into position first. Bolan's armorplated rig was well suited to this task, and he made steady progress through the streets.

The warrior drove by the U.S. embassy. Stone walls surrounded the neat, dignified building. The barrier wouldn't stop any determined opponent. The embassy was a fat, easy victim for anyone ruthless enough to go for it.

Traffic came to a standstill because a wide truck had overheated and stalled in the middle of the street. Horns blared and voices shouted curses in Spanish and English. Pedestrians took advantage of the situation to cross the street. They slipped between vehicles, some sliding across hoods or trunks to the dismay of the drivers. Many of the pedestrians seemed pleased, perhaps because people with more money than they had now suffered some inconvenience due to their expensive machines.

Drastic differences in social status were obvious. The people with means clearly flaunted their wealth among the lower-class majority. The Mexican middle class had grown in recent years, yet most still lived at a standard that would be considered below the poverty line in the United States. Street merchants approached the stationary vehicles with bundles of blankets, cheap pottery and assorted items. Beggars staggered forward with outstretched hands and grim faces.

Bolan recalled one of Karl Brunje's minihistory lessons from a previous meeting with the CIA man. He mentioned that armies of lepers had roamed the streets of Mexico City in the seventeenth century, when it was known as the capital of New Spain. These *leprosos* were basically beggars and thrust out diseased hands with missing fingers for alms. They found little comfort for their suffering aside from strong drink, and occasionally mobs of drunken *leprosos* went on sprees of violence and riots.

Leprosy was no longer a problem in Mexico City, but the despair of the ultrapoor remained. Bolan had also noticed the beggars appeared to be Indians, while the majority of the upper class in Mexico City tended to be pale-skinned with a racial heritage that suggested a European bloodline rather than mestizo. It wasn't hard to understand why the Indian poor would resent the rich and distrust the government. No wonder they suspected the North American Free Trade Agreement was just a scheme by the fat cats in Mexico and America to benefit themselves while cutting off even more opportunities to the poor.

Emiliano Zapata had formed his army of would-be revolutionaries from the ranks of the poor Indian populations in 1910. The modern-day rebels who bore his name sprang from the same source, and Adolfo Valdez had created his own terrorist forces by capitalizing on the anger and hatred born of the misery and poverty of the Indian lower class.

The traffic jam ended as the truck finally moved forward. Bolan was relieved to leave the congregation of beggars. There was nothing he could do about their plight. Insight into the reason anyone would be drawn to join Valdez's terrorist movement was only useful if this could help him stop the enemy. He might sympathize with conditions that caused people to act in desperation and rage, but that didn't excuse wanton destruction or the murder of innocent people.

Bolan found a reserved parking space behind a hardware store roughly two hundred yards from the embassy. He took the aluminum cases from the van, locked the vehicle and headed for a door marked NO ENTRE. The warrior pressed a buzzer button and waited.

The door opened, and a lean young man with black hair, broad features and nut-brown skin greeted Bolan with a blank stare. Another face appeared at the man's right shoulder, identical to the first, as if the person had suddenly grown another head. On the second face a bland expression changed to a sly grin.

"Buenas tardes, señor," he declared. *"Sírvase entrar."*

The pair stepped aside. They were the same height and build. Both wore white shirts, but one man's pants were black and the other's blue. Bolan entered as Miguel Santos appeared. The Executioner was glad to see a familiar face, especially one that didn't appear to be part of a secret cloning operation.

"Hello, Mr. Belasko," Santos said. "You met my cousins, Ramon and Raul. They're twins."

"Really?" Bolan replied dryly. "Nice to meet you. *Mucho gusto en conocerle."*

The twins smiled. The man in blue spoke. "Don't worry, Mr. Belasko. We speak English. I'm Ramon and this is Raul."

The other man nodded.

"They own this store," Santos explained. "They also work with me on assignments. Family is the best loyalty you can have, eh? Raul and Ramon are very good with electrical devices, including those used for eavesdropping and surveillance."

"Good. We can use their help. I have some more equipment and a special vehicle for us as well."

Bolan glanced at the shelves of tools, boxes of nails, sacks of chemical fertilizer and assorted appliances. A pump-action shotgun stood in a corner. Large keys contained pieces of metal pipe. Rope and electrical cords wrapped in coils were hung on wall pegs.

"My friends in the police department have been notified to expect another terrorist incident in the city," Santos stated. "I've warned them that an escalated police presence might cause a greater risk because the terrorists are loco and might use extreme measures. They've formed a special antiterrorist unit, similar to your SWAT team in the United States. These elite police officers are already on call in case of another emergency after the Henderson assassination."

"Just bear in mind we need the roadblocks more than a SWAT team," Bolan said. "We can't let Valdez get away again."

"You say this as if you are quite certain he'll attack the embassy," Raul commented. "Aren't we concentrating all our efforts on this possibility while Valdez might plan to strike elsewhere?"

"Yeah," Bolan admitted, "but I'm pretty sure we're barking up the right tree. Sorry about the slang expression."

"We understand what you mean," Santos assured him. "We can use this store as a safehouse. That is the expression?"

"Yeah, that's right. This place will be an ideal temporary base of operations because it's located close to the embassy. But you'll have to close the business until this is over."

"We already did that," Ramon replied. "Miguel assured us we'd receive more than ample financial consideration to compensate for the time we'd be unable to make profit in the usual manner here."

"You do speak English well," Bolan remarked. "We'll need somewhere to sleep in shifts. It will be best if we can prepare food here as well."

"We have an apartment over the store," Raul told him. "Sometimes one or both of us stay here overnight. Sometimes it's a good place to bring a woman...."

"*He* brings women here," Ramon interjected. "I'm married. Don't start rumors that I commit adultery, Raul."

"Belasko isn't here to check on your behavior," Santos stated. "I've been to the apartment. It has everything we'll need, including a kitchen and two beds."

"Great," Bolan said. "We get set up immediately. We need to establish shifts, prepare for surveillance and communication with home base and the men in the field. We also need more vehicles. The terrorists will soon get suspicious if they see that gray van too often."

"We can use at least three other automobiles," Santos replied.

"What about weapons? You guys need to be armed with something you know how to use."

"We have pistol permits," Santos answered. "Not easy to get here in Mexico City, but it pays to have friends among the police and Feds. We can also use rifles similar to the Marlin you regard as undesirable. Did you get that fancy military assault rifle yet?"

"No," Bolan answered. "No more grenades either. And the M-203 launcher and 40 mm shells didn't arrive."

He pointed at the pump shotgun in the corner and said, "How many shotguns can we get? It's a hell of a good weapon at close quarters."

"We can get more shotguns," Santos assured him. "I don't need to tell you that a shotgun may be excellent at close quarters, but it has very limited range."

"Yeah, but it has considerably more range if one fires a solid slug or deer slayer instead of buckshot. We could use solid slugs as well as double-O-buckshot. There are also some tricks that can be done with shotgun shells. Pellets can be strung together to form grapeshot."

"Grapeshot?" Ramon inquired with a puzzled expression.

"It was used by both sides during the Civil War in the U.S. The shotgun pellets are connected by wire to prevent the buckshot from spreading. The effect is to hit the target with a cluster of pellets—each about the size of a 7.62 mm bullet—all set close together. You can imagine what sort of damage that would do to human flesh and bone."

"I hope I won't have to see this for myself," Santos remarked. "Just the picture in my imagination is bad enough."

"It's not pretty," Bolan confirmed, "but it works. You can also increase the penetration force of a solid slug by fitting a common BB to the nose of the slug. Shotgun shells can be turned into minigrenades that explode on impact."

The warrior approached the keg filled with metal pipes. He removed one piece of pipe roughly fifteen inches long. Bolan glanced at the racks of nails and cords of rope. The other men watched, confused and curious about the big American's actions.

"We can make some explosives," he announced. "And we can even come up with a grenade launcher. Not exactly high-tech, but it'll work."

"I think maybe I'm glad we don't get customers like you in here all the time," Ramon remarked.

MACK BOLAN SAT at the table and fitted a shotgun shell into a short plastic tube. It had to be fixed in place before a cork with a nail could be set at the bottom. The nail point touched the primer at the base of the shell and would serve as a firing pin when the nail head struck a solid surface. The other end of the plastic tube was cut into a frilled fan to make certain the nail end would be heavier and the contraption would land properly to go off.

Bolan finished the shotgun-shell minigrenade and placed it in a cardboard box with several others. He had been working on the project for hours. The warrior seldom had to improvise weaponry in the field, and he found the chore annoying because he had been forced to do so due to blundering by some faceless morons in the CIA. Yet he found it relaxing after a while. It was similar to tying fly hooks for fishing or preparing cartridges with reloading gear as he had as a young man.

The apartment was small, but comfortable. Bolan had the place to himself during the day because he had elected to take the graveyard shift for the surveillance on the embassy. A special communications computer unit was set up to keep him in touch with Stony Man Farm and with Karl Brunjes at the embassy. He had already reported what information he had to Brognola. There had been little the big Fed could add to the mission except to assure the soldier they would find the problem with the supply line and take care of it. However, the M-16 and other weaponry had yet to arrive at the embassy, and Bolan would have to assume it wouldn't be on hand when he next confronted Valdez and his people.

The Executioner had no doubt Valdez would personally participate in the attack on the embassy. The renegade's personality would compel him to take part in such an important and dangerous operation. Valdez couldn't allow anyone else to command the assault force against the embassy. He had come to Mexico and formed the terrorist legions because he was driven by anger and resentment toward the United States of America, not because he cared what happened to oppressed Indians or other disadvantaged Mexican citizens. Valdez wouldn't want to miss this target because it meant too much to him.

That was what Bolan figured, and he was very good at guessing what an opponent might do... especially an opponent who probably thought and acted in a manner similar to himself. There were obvious differences between Bolan and Valdez, but he knew it wouldn't help to dwell on those traits. The warrior didn't worry about his character or motivations. He needed to try to understand Valdez in order to "read" the man and try to extrapolate what the enemy's action would be.

Bolan knew he wasn't a mind reader and couldn't guess every move an opponent might make. He didn't waste time and energy trying to figure out every possible detail to every minute degree. So he tried to relax and rest until the time for action occurred. He wore only a pair of khaki pants and an undershirt as he sat at the table. His Israeli Desert Eagle sat on the table within easy reach, but that was due to habit rather than a genuine concern about danger. Bolan felt as safe as he could expect to be during a mission.

A buzzer sounded, announcing someone at the door downstairs. Bolan rose and shoved the pistol into his waistband at the small of his back. He glanced at a Remington pump shotgun in a corner, considered taking it and decided it probably wouldn't be necessary. He padded barefoot down the stairs to the storage room, reached the door and peered through the peephole.

Ellena Santos stood outside. Bolan unlocked and opened the door, admitting the young woman. She smiled as Bolan closed and locked the door.

"Hope I didn't wake you," she said.

"I was awake," Bolan assured her. "There's some coffee on. Do you want a cup?"

"Rather have something cold," Ellena replied. "It's hot outside. I passed the embassy on the way here. Thought I saw the van."

They mounted the stairs, Ellena leading the way.

"Ramon and Raul have the vehicle," Bolan explained. "They really like that rig. The armor plating and various gadgets are new to them and they seem to enjoy using the van."

"Like something from a James Bond movie?" Ellena asked, smiling as she glanced over a shoulder at Bolan.

"Something like that. I've used that sort of high-tech surveillance gear so many times in the past I'm a little jaded now."

They reached the upstairs section and entered the apartment. Ellena moved to the table and turned to face Bolan.

"What else has lost its novelty for you?" she asked. "Have missions like this one become old hat?"

The warrior shrugged. "You can never get used to this sort of thing. I do what I do because it needs to be done. Each situation is different."

Bolan headed for the refrigerator. He offered his visitor beer, juice or soda. Ellena selected orange juice, and he poured her a glass while she glanced at the minigrenades in the box.

"Careful," he warned. "If one of those strikes the floor or table on the nail head, it'll go off."

She backed away from the box without touching it.

"Is this how you've been spending your spare time?"

"Keeps me off the streets," Bolan replied. "Here's your juice."

"May I sit down, or do you have the chairs rigged to explode as well?"

"Go ahead," Bolan said. "I haven't gotten around to booby-trapping the furniture yet."

Ellena sat in a chair and sipped her juice. She looked around the room and noticed Bolan's shotgun. A canvas bag and three thin sticks, each almost a yard long, stood near the weapon.

"Another project of yours?" she asked.

"Yeah," Bolan replied. "The bag contains some pipe bombs. Simple explosive. Oversize firecrackers. These can be used as improvised grenades or attached to one of those sticks and fired from the shotgun as a crude grenade launcher."

"Fired from a shotgun?" Ellena asked with surprise.

"You use a shotgun shell prepared for the purpose," Bolan answered. "Open the end, remove the buckshot and pack cotton over the gunpowder charge. The shell casing has to remain open so it has to be placed into the breech manually...this is probably boring."

"No," Ellena insisted. "Go on."

Bolan moved to the sticks by the shotgun. He raised one and held an end near the muzzle of the Remington as he spoke.

"Okay," Bolan continued. "A stick with a pipe bomb attached is inserted down the barrel to the open shell and cotton wadding. Then you light the fuse to the bomb, pick your target before it goes off and take aim. Trigger the shotgun and the powder charge propels the stick and the bomb like a javelin with an explosive warhead."

"Are you sure that will work?"

"It works," Bolan assured her. "Not as well as a real grenade launcher, but it's the best we can come up with under the circumstances."

"I hope you won't have to use something like that in a crowded area," Ellena said. "There are generally a lot of people near the embassy."

"We won't use explosives unless we have to. That'll be up to the terrorists. If we're lucky, they'll carry out the attack when it's late. Say, three o'clock in the morning."

"That's when you think Valdez will attack?" she asked. "That's why you took that shift for your watch, isn't it?"

Bolan shrugged and said, "I hope Valdez will be concerned about the lives of innocent bystanders and try to hit the place when there's fewer people around. Good chance he will. After all, thick traffic will also make a getaway difficult."

"I'm not surprised you would choose to put yourself at greater risk than the others," Ellena said with unfettered admiration.

"I have more experience at this sort of thing," the warrior replied.

"When this is over you'll be going back to the United States. We'll probably never see you again."

"Never know how things might work out in the future," Bolan said. "Still, things will get back to normal, and you and your brother will be able to get back to your lives the way they were before this all happened."

"Yes," she said without enthusiasm. "The way they were before. Actually I came here to bring you some photographs of individuals spotted near the embassy who seemed unusually interested in it."

She opened her purse and removed a large yellow envelope. Bolan approached as Ellena placed it on the table. She extracted several photos and computer printout sheets.

"We've identified three persons as men with criminal records," Ellena explained. "If I remember correctly, one went to prison for armed robbery and the other two were convicted for assault. Two other individuals in the photographs participated in a demonstration against the government's support of NAFTA several months before it actually went into effect. They were obviously Zapatista sympathizers, so a file was kept on them because they might prove to be enemies of the state."

"I'm usually not thrilled with the 'big brother' attitude by any government," Bolan remarked, "but this time it seems to play in our favor."

"It also proves your theory might be right," Ellena said. "Not much room for doubt that the terrorists intend to attack the embassy."

He tried to keep his attention on the evidence Ellena had placed on the table, but his eyes were drawn to her. The woman was quite a distraction. Her eyes seemed bright and expressive, her lips designed for passion.

"Have you ever heard the expression that people do not regret what they did in life as much as those things they did not do?" she asked.

"Yeah," Bolan replied. "It might be true, but I try not to do anything I might regret or others might regret later."

"I don't think either of us will regret making love," Ellena said bluntly, "but we would both be sorry if we failed to do so and never had another chance."

"Ellena," the Executioner said, "I'm not going to argue with that."

He leaned closer, and she lifted her head for his kiss.

6

"I think these precautions are getting a bit excessive," the ambassador for the United States complained.

"Luis Donaldo Colosio might have said the same if his security people had demanded he exercised greater personal safety while campaigning in Tijuana during March 1994," Karl Brunjes replied.

"Colosio was shot in the head," the ambassador remarked. "A bulletproof vest wouldn't have saved him."

"He was also shot at close range with a handgun," the CIA officer pointed out. "We're going to try to keep you far enough from any potential assassins to prevent that. Of course, a rifle marksman won't have to get very close to make an accurate head shot."

"That's encouraging," the ambassador said dryly.

"I just want you to take this seriously, Mr. Ambassador," Brunjes explained.

The pair walked from the embassy building to a long black limousine parked in the driveway. Brunjes felt as awkward as the ambassador, clad in a Kevlar vest under his shirt and with the unfamiliar weight of a Magnum revolver holstered under his arm. At that moment he felt rather foolish. They had prepared for trouble the past three days because Belasko—or whatever his real name was—had predicted that terrorists would attack the embassy. How much longer would this continue before something happened to either confirm or disprove this claim?

So far the only suspicious evidence to support Belasko's theory had been a couple photographs of some ex-convicts strolling by the embassy. Mexico had prisons and most inmates were eventually released. Brunjes didn't know how many ex-cons might be living in or even passing through Mexico City at any given day, but the size of the population probably included thousands of men who had served time. They might be geared up for a threat that didn't even exist beyond Belasko's paranoid imagination.

The CIA officer and the ambassador reached the car. Two Marines stood by the front gate as it slowly opened with a mechanical buzz. The sentries were smartly dressed in blue class-A uniform with polished brass, white service caps and gloves. Yet the pistols in their button-flap holsters were loaded and assault rifles were stored in their guard shack by the gate. They stood solemnly as the gate opened and the ambassador prepared to enter his vehicle.

Then Brunjes saw the truck.

It was a battered old pickup, not unlike hundreds found throughout the country. Several men sat in the back of the vehicle, dressed as laborers with straw hats and sunglasses. Brunjes might have ignored the truck, although it slowed to a crawl by the embassy, had he not been alert to possible danger. The passengers pulled neckerchiefs onto their faces to cover noses and mouths.

"Down!" the CIA man roared.

The ambassador didn't respond and failed to realize the threat. Brunjes reached inside his jacket for the revolver with one hand and grabbed the ambassador's shoulder with the other. He pulled the diplomat's jacket and swept a foot to the back of the man's ankle. The ambassador cried out in surprise as he suddenly lost his balance and fell on his backside.

Brunjes carried out the simple judo trip-throw smoothly, years of martial-arts training riding with his reflexes better than he would have expected. However, he was less familiar with firearms and he found drawing the big Magnum gun from shoulder leather awkward: The front sight snagged on his jacket as Brunjes saw the men in the truck produce rifles and submachine guns.

He dropped to one knee and ducked behind the limo as automatic gunfire erupted. Brunjes cleared the .357 revolver from his jacket and glanced at the startled face of the ambassador. Metal hammered metal and the limo trembled from the impact. The enemy was shooting at them. Brunjes gripped the revolver with both hands.

"Stay down!" he told the ambassador.

"Don't worry about that," was the reply.

He crept to the rear of the limo and carefully peered over the top, exposing no more of his head than necessary. One Marine lay on the ground, his body riddled with bullet holes. The other managed to reach the shack and fired his pistol at the gang of terrorists. No doubt he was trying to get to the assault rifles, but two enemy gunmen sprayed the shed with twin salvos of full-auto rounds. The Marine convulsed in agony and fell against a window inside the shed. Glass shattered and the dead man's upper torso draped the windowsill.

"Jesus," Brunjes rasped. "Where the hell is Belasko?"

MACK BOLAN STOOD on the Ford Mustang's accelerator. The car had been provided by Santos and the twins. It was at least fifteen years old, and something rattled inside the engine as Bolan sped through the streets to the embassy. Santos had contacted him at the safehouse. The investigator said the embassy was under attack, and Bolan immediately grabbed his gear and headed for the combat zone.

Vehicles and pedestrians bolted from the direction of the embassy. Bolan swerved the Mustang clear of some panicked runners and hit the horn to warn others. He heard gunfire and knew the conflict was still in progress. The warrior held the wheel with one hand and quickly slipped a bandolier loaded with shotgun shells across his shoulder.

He had donned a field jacket over his undershirt. The pockets bulged with shotgun-shell minigrenades, and spare magazines for the .44 Magnum Desert Eagle had been thrust in his waistband. The Executioner had left the safehouse so quickly he hadn't bothered to put on boots and wore only a pair of slip-on loafers. Yet, he hadn't forgotten the Remington shotgun in his haste or the canvas bag loaded with pipe bombs.

As the warrior approached the embassy, he saw the pickup truck by the gate. Gunmen by the entrance exchanged fire with Marines at the main building and at someone positioned by a limo in the driveway. Across the street, Santos knelt by another parked car and fired at the terrorists with a lever-action rifle. Bolan spotted at least three slain terrorists on the pavement. He didn't know how many losses the other side had suffered, but the enemy appeared to be well armed, and he was certain the killers by the gate were only part of the attack force.

His suspicions were confirmed when more figures appeared on the street. Neckerchief masks clearly labeled them as terrorists. They used parked vehicles, lampposts and public benches for cover as they approached. Some fired weapons, most aimed at the embassy. Others waited to move into better positions before participating in the fight.

Fortunately civilians had bolted from the scene of the battle. Some had abandoned their cars to flee on foot, probably afraid they wouldn't be able to escape through heavy traffic. Bolan didn't see any innocent bystanders in the line of fire as he steered the Mustang around a Ford in the middle of the street and headed for Santos's position. The investigator was preoccupied with the exchange between himself and the hardmen by the front of the embassy. He hadn't noticed Bolan's arrival or a pair of masked figures who approached him on foot.

The stealthy pair crept closer, using available cover to conceal their movement. Bolan almost hit the horn, but realized this would only draw Santos's attention toward the Mustang rather than warn him of danger from the two terrorists. The warrior turned sharply and the front tires of his vehicle hopped the curb and he stomped the brake. He opened the door and slid out, Desert Eagle in his fist.

"Belasko!" Santos called out in recognition.

"Behind you!" Bolan shouted.

Santos's eyes widened with surprise and fear. He turned, jacking the lever action to his rifle as he swung it toward the new threat. The terrorist gunmen froze in place, also startled, although the neckerchief and dark glasses hid their expressions. One raised an FAL assault rifle to his shoulder and took aim. Santos thrust his Marlin forward like a magic wand. The investigator pulled the trigger and the rifle responded without mystical powers, but launched a .30-30 slug by the earthbound principles of physics, chemistry and kinetics.

The bullet plowed into the upper torso of the enemy rifleman a split second before the terrorist fired his weapon. A burst of 7.62 mm rounds slashed across Santos's extended arm and shoulder. He cried out as the Marlin spun from his grasp. His shattered arm dropped, blood streamed from multiple wounds. Yet the terrorist Santos had shot also dropped his weapon, and fell to his knees, his expression twisted by pain and the knowledge he had failed to take out the investigator. Mortally wounded, the gunman slumped to the pavement.

Whatever sense of victory Santos enjoyed at that moment was short-lived. The second terrorist pointed his M-3 subgun at the investigator and fired. Several .45-caliber rounds smashed into Santos's body and lifted him off his feet to land heavily on the ground. The recoil of the large caliber, blow-back action "grease gun" raised the barrel to the sky as the killer gazed down at his victim.

Bolan seized the opportunity and snap-aimed his Desert Eagle. With skill and instincts developed by years of training and experience, the Executioner fired a single, well-placed round. The big .44 Magnum missile punched through the neckerchief mask and blasted a gory exit at the back of the gunman's skull. The terrorist collapsed beside the still body of his slain comrade.

Bolan resisted the urge to rush to Santos and check the investigator on the slim chance he might still be alive. The embassy was still under attack and several terrorists remained. The warrior headed back to the Mustang to get the rest of his weaponry. A salvo of enemy bullets pelted the hood and windshield as he lunged inside the vehicle. Obviously Bolan's arrival hadn't been overlooked and the terrorists had added his termination to their agenda for the day.

Fair enough, Bolan thought as he sprawled across the front seat. Glass cracked, but the windshield held together. The warrior kept his head down and grabbed the canvas bag. He opened the door on the passenger side, seized the Remington shotgun and slithered out to the sidewalk. Bolan used the shotgun barrel to shove the door shut and rolled on his side. Voices shouted amid the roar of gunfire. He couldn't understand what was said, but he realized the voices came from the opposite side of the car and belonged to someone only three or four yards from his position.

Bolan put down the shotgun and reached into a pocket with one hand, the Desert Eagle still in his other fist. He withdrew four minigrenades and heaved them over the top of the Mustang toward the enemy voices. The Executioner remained alert to the possibility that terrorists might attempt a two-prong attack. That vigilance saved his life when a masked hardman advanced by the nose of the car. The terrorists had hoped to catch Bolan preoccupied by the gunfire from the other shooters. A .44 Magnum round and the thunderous bellow of the big pistol announced this plan had failed. The would-be assassin stopped the bullet with his chest and staggered backward, unable to bring his own MAC-10 Ingram to play.

Bolan heard the minigrenades explode on impact with the pavement even as he shot the ambusher with a second Magnum slug to be certain he would go down and stay down. Screams proved the buckshot from the improvised grenades had claimed human flesh. Bolan scooped up the Remington as he got to his feet and thrust the Eagle into his waistband. The hot metal against the thin fabric of his undershirt made his abdomen twitch, but Bolan hardly noticed as he peered across the hood of the Mustang and raised the shotgun with both hands.

Two masked figures stumbled on unsteady legs. Their limbs and torsos had been torn and bloodied by buckshot from the minigrenade blasts. The terrorists had been surprised by the Executioner's counterattack. Although seriously wounded, neither man was down and both raised their subguns. Bolan pointed the Remington and squeezed the trigger. A 12-gauge burst sent the closer hardman to the ground in a lifeless heap. The Executioner pumped the Remington, ejected the spent shell casing and chambered another round as he trained the weapon on the second terrorist. Wormlike intestines bulged from a wound in the man's belly and his body convulsed in pain. Bolan ended his suffering forever with a shotgun blast to the chest.

The immediate threat to Bolan's life dispelled, he turned his attention to the terrorist siege on the embassy. The enemy had discovered crossing the threshold or even firing through the open gate to be more difficult than anticipated. The Marines effectively kept the terrorists at bay with a constant wave of full-automatic fire. To compound the enemy's problems, the steel gate began to slide shut, operated by the electrical system inside the building.

Frustrated, a terrorist lobbed a hand grenade over the wall. It exploded on embassy grounds, splattering the limo with clumps of dirt and shrapnel. Another attacker thrust the barrel of his rifle between the bars to the gate and fired a short burst. His head violently jerked sideways and he slumped along the gate to the ground, his corpse serving as a warning to the others that the defense forces inside the compound were still alert to danger.

"Move out of the way!" a voice shouted from the street.

The angry command in English, followed by a vulgar Spanish version, drew Bolan's attention. He saw a tall figure advance from between a pair of parked cars. Although the man wore a cap and dark glasses, no neckerchief covered his lower face. Bolan was certain he was Valdez. Under stress, the guy had spoken in English—which was the language he had most used in his life despite his decision to abandon the United States.

The terrorist commander carried an M-79 grenade launcher in his fists and an H&K MP-5 strapped to his back. Three other assassins accompanied Valdez. The smallest member of the group held a G-3 rifle at chest level. Baggy clothing and a mask didn't conceal the fact the terrorist was female. The Executioner wished women wouldn't join such extremist groups. He didn't enjoy killing and especially disliked killing women. Still, a well-armed female was as dangerous as her male counterpart and would have to be dealt with in the same manner. Bullets delivered the ultimate, ruthless form of equal opportunity.

Bolan jogged to Santos's vehicle for cover. He glanced down at the investigator's body. Blood had ceased to leak from the wounds, which suggested the heart no longer pumped. Bullet holes in the chest and abdomen revealed he had been hit in at least two vital organs. The Executioner no longer had the slightest doubt Santos was dead.

There was no time to spare mourning his slain ally. Bolan hurried along the vehicles to reach Valdez's position. He had to get within range to effectively use the Remington shotgun or the Desert Eagle to stop the deadly foursome. Valdez pointed the M-79 at the closed gates to the embassy as the warrior drew closer.

The female terrorist turned suddenly, spotted Bolan and swung her weapon toward him. The Executioner triggered the Remington and blasted the woman with a burst of double-O buckshot before she could fire her G-3. Bolan triggered his launcher at the same instant, abruptly spinning and dropping the M-79 even as the 40 mm grenade shell exploded.

A blast of heavy explosive smashed the metal barrier to the embassy. The gate collapsed in a heap of tangled bars and concrete dust. Several terrorists returned to the threshold and once more attempted to assault the embassy, spraying the compound with automatic-weapons fire as they tried to rush their objective.

Valdez didn't join the charge. He clasped his left hand to his inner right forearm and glared at Bolan through his dark glasses. Stray buckshot had struck him and forced the enemy commander to drop his grenade launcher. The female terrorist lay dead near his feet, but the remaining pair of hardmen immediately turned their weapons toward the Executioner.

Bolan jacked the pump Remington as he ducked for cover at the nose of a parked Chevy, abandoned in the middle of the street. A volley of gunfire chased the warrior, slugs punching a line of holes in the body-work. The Executioner whipped the shotgun barrel across the hood without exposing himself. Bolan fired the weapon without aiming, not expecting to hit the enemy, trying only to keep them at bay.

He stayed low and moved along the length of the vehicle. Bolan risked a look from his new position as he drew the Desert Eagle. He saw a gunman stagger on unsteady legs, rifle in hand although his right side was peppered by pellet wounds. The shotgun blast had scored better than the warrior had expected. He aimed quickly and fired the .44 pistol as the enemy gunner brought his weapon to bear. A high-velocity round crashed into the side of the man's face, sliced through his skull and left a fist-sized exit wound.

The second terrorist whirled and swung his weapon toward Bolan, who triggered the big pistol twice. Both .44 slugs hit the gunman in the center of the chest, the impacts hurling him to the ground in a bloodied heap alongside the other fallen attackers. Bolan scanned the area. The M-79 grenade launcher lay on the pavement, but Adolfo Valdez was gone.

The Executioner searched for the missing terrorist leader among the other vehicles and surrounding cover. He didn't see Valdez, but three of his henchmen turned their attention and firearms to the warrior's position. Bolan glimpsed the muzzles of their weapons, jutting along the frame of a four-door Ford, and dropped to one knee behind the shelter of the Chevy. Streams of automatic fire erupted and tore into the metal body of the car, the vehicle vibrating from the force of the high-velocity slugs.

He knew he couldn't remain there for long. The enemy would soon take advantage of the situation and either attempt to attack from a different direction or lob grenades at the Chevy. Bolan reached into the canvas bag and removed a pipe bomb. He took a cigarette lighter from a pocket, struck the wheel and held the flame to the stubby fuse at the capped end of the bomb. Sparks sputtered as the fuse burned rapidly.

Bolan hurled the improvised explosive over the top of the car, toward the enemy trio. The pipe hit the pavement and rolled to the Ford, exploding with a roar. The blast ripped apart the vehicle and the gunmen behind it. Chunks of metal, plastic and human body parts hurtled in all directions. Gasoline burst into flames to create an impromptu crematorium in the middle of the street.

A vehicle lunged forward, crashed into the side of a small Volkswagen to knock it aside with ease. Bolan recognized the big gray van. Bullets whined against the armored hull without effect. Ramon or Raul steered the rig. The warrior didn't know which face was behind the reinforced glass of the windshield, but he was glad to see the twins and the CIA special vehicle. The other brother appeared at the rear of the van, clutching a Marlin rifle.

The van was the best, strongest available cover. Bolan scooped up the canvas bag and the Remington and headed for the rig. He sprinted to the vehicle as the driver's door opened.

"Glad to see you, Ramon," he said.

"Raul," the twin replied.

"Yeah," Bolan said. "That's what I meant. Santos is dead."

"¡Madre de Dios! Are you certain?"

"I'm sure," Bolan replied. "Where the hell are the cops? Did you radio for backup?"

"Yes. We were patrolling the area when the shooting started. Ramon tried to contact you before calling for the police. Then we turned the corner and ran into half a dozen terrorists, who blocked the street with two cars. We required a few minutes to get through them. Shot a couple of them and ran over one or two when we broke through to get here."

"Move the van to the front of the embassy," Bolan instructed. "Park beside the entrance, not right in front of it, or we might get hit by friendly fire from inside the embassy grounds."

Raul nodded. He called to his brother. "Let's go, Ramon!"

Ramon climbed inside the rear of the vehicle as Raul got behind the steering wheel. Bolan ran alongside the van as it moved forward. Gunfire continued to pelt the armored rig. A grenade exploded and showered the van with shrapnel. A direct hit by a heavy explosive could take them out, regardless of the reinforced metal hull.

Bolan knew Valdez was still alive. The man had been wounded, but the buckshot tears in their leader's arm didn't appear serious to the Executioner. The limb was certainly hurt, but that probably wouldn't stop a determined opponent like Valdez. He had no doubt retreated to command his ranks to deal with the unexpected arrival of Bolan and the battle wagon. At least he had dropped the M-79 grenade launcher. Bolan hoped Valdez hadn't packed a spare for the occasion.

The van hopped the curb near the embassy. A heap of slain hardmen littered the entrance by the gate, yet gunfire announced the defensive forces on the grounds still had their hands full. Sirens screamed in the distance, announcing the arrival of the police. The terrorists would have heard the sirens as well and would realize they had to make one last attempt to take out the embassy before being forced to run.

Bolan moved to the rear of the van and carefully peered around the edge to see what strategy the enemy would try next. Only two opponents fired assault rifles at the rig, and it appeared to be only strafing fire, intended to keep the warrior and the twins down while the rest of the terrorists prepared the real attack. The majority of the remaining enemy force seemed to have congregated among a cluster of motionless, bullet-scarred vehicles. Valdez had called for a huddle, like the captain of a football team planning a final desperate play.

"Raul! Ramon!" Bolan demanded. "One of you get me a couple of those pipe bombs on sticks! Make it quick!"

The Executioner pumped the shotgun to eject the remaining shells from the magazine tube. He left the chamber open and selected a shell from his bandolier, marked by a small white X on the brass. The top of the shell was open, and Bolan glanced inside the plastic hood to be certain the cotton wadding remained in place over the charge inside. He placed it into the Remington's chamber as one of the twins appeared with two long sticks, each mounted with a pipe-bomb warhead.

"Great," Bolan said with a nod. "Stay alert. They won't like what happens next."

The Executioner inserted a stick down the barrel of the shotgun as he spoke, making certain the end of the pole fitted into the open end of the shotgun shell before he jacked the chamber shut. The pipe bomb weaved near the muzzle of the weapon as Bolan braced the buttstock to a hip. He judged the distance to the enemy lair, aimed and canted the barrel slightly to compensate for the trajectory of the unconventional projectile. He told the twins to light the fuse. Raul struck a match and held it to the pipe bomb.

The fuse ignited and began to burn. Bolan sucked in a short, tense breath and squeezed the trigger. The Remington recoiled forcibly against his hip as a low-throated bellow erupted from the barrel. The stick sailed high and rocketed for the terrorist position. Startled voices cried out in alarm when the enemy spotted the blurred shape above them.

Figures scrambled as the stick grenade descended, dropping from view by the group of vehicles. A sudden blast knocked two cars sideways and hurled three bodies into the sky. Smashed and broken figures crashed to the pavement as flames rose from burning gasoline.

A shape bolted forward, trailing fire, shrieking in pain and horror. A quick mercy round from a comrade put the man out of his misery. Other terrorists staggered from the fiery wreckage, bloodied and wounded by shrapnel. Bolan drew his Desert Eagle and brought down one injured opponent with a well-placed .44 Magnum round. The twins' rifles roared, and two more enemies fell.

Two automobiles and a pickup truck suddenly came to life and sped from the battleground. A fourth vehicle lunged forward, the panicked driver unaware or unconcerned that the car was pointed toward Bolan and the van. The Executioner reached into a pocket as the Chevy approached and hurled a pair of minigrenades at the nose of the car. The shotgun shells burst on impact with the pavement. Buckshot tore into the front tires and the engine block. The hood popped open as the Chevy spun out of control, crashing sideways into the Mustang Bolan had driven to the scene. Metal crunched and the windshield burst as the head and shoulders of a terrorist passenger punched through the glass.

KARL BRUNJES OPENED the cylinder of his S&W revolver and shook out the spent .357 Magnum shell casings. The CIA officer had emptied his weapon into the horde of terrorists that swarmed through the smashed front gate. Several dead hardmen littered the lawn.

"Is it over?" the ambassador asked.

The diplomat sat on the ground, back pressed against a rear tire, hands clasped together in a manner between a prayer and tense rage. Brunjes knelt by the side of the limo, reluctant to raise his head. He was aware at least one of the bullet-resistant windows of the big black car had shattered from prolonged hammering by high-velocity slugs to kill the driver. The man's brains splattered the inside of the windshield.

Yet the CIA man realized the shooting and explosions had stopped. The wail of sirens drew closer and he noticed the Marines had lowered their weapons, although they remained by the cover of the main building. He sighed with relief, closed the cylinder to the Magnum and placed the gun on the ground.

A shape materialized at the nose of the limo. Brunjes gazed up at the figure. Clad in work clothes, shirtfront splashed with blood, the terrorist advanced on shaky limbs. His dark glasses and straw hat had been lost, and the neckerchief hung loose from the man's face. Pink froth drooled from his open mouth, the result of a bullet-pierced lung. Yet, his eyes expressed fury and hatred as he pointed a large bowie knife at Brunjes.

"Oh, shit!" the ambassador shouted.

He voiced Brunjes's feeling as the CIA man rose to meet the charge. The blade slashed and Brunjes jumped back. Sharp steel cut across his shirt at abdomen level and raked the protective Kevlar vest. The

CIA officer didn't give the terrorist another chance. He quickly grabbed the wrist above the knife with one hand and the man's elbow with the other, then stepped forward, with the motion of the knifeman's stroke. He locked the arm and increased his opponent's momentum to drive the man forcibly into the steel frame of the limo.

Brunjes twisted the wrist and hammered his other fist into the captive forearm to jar the ulna nerve. The knife dropped from limp fingers. The terrorist violently shoved away from the car to break free of his captor's grasp. The CIA officer let go, but instantly thrust a heel-of-palm stroke under the man's jaw. The blow stunned his adversary, and Brunjes closed in and seized the man's arm.

He raised the limb and turned to plant his shoulder into the terrorist's armpit. Brunjes bent his knees to lift the man, then straightened his legs and bent his waist to hurl the guy overhead in a classic judo shoulder throw. The man hit the ground hard and lay on his back, eyes glazed from the punishment. Brunjes stomped a heel into his opponent's chest. Ribs caved in under his foot, and a glob of blood was vomited from the fallen terrorist's mouth.

"Jesus!" the CIA man gasped.

Brunjes retreated from the still form, aware he had killed the man. He covered his mouth with a hand, afraid he might throw up, and glanced across the hood of the limo to see Mack Bolan approach.

"You all right, Karl?" the warrior asked.

Brunjes nodded in reply.

"The embassy is still standing," Bolan observed. "How's the ambassador?"

Another nod.

"Reckon I'll talk to you later," the Executioner decided.

7

Hal Brognola sat at the conference table in the Stony Man War Room, listening to Mack Bolan report on what had happened in Mexico City. The Executioner's image appeared on the wall screen.

"We're not certain how many terrorists managed to escape," Bolan explained. "Probably a dozen or so. They chose a street route that avoided most of the police headed for the embassy. Valdez did his homework. He obviously had a pretty good idea which streets the cops would use based on which would be the fastest routes to the embassy."

"I thought Santos was supposed to emphasize the need for roadblocks when he contacted the police about preparations in case the terrorists attacked?" the big Fed remarked.

"He did," Bolan said. "Santos couldn't force the police to follow strategy we wanted. They still seemed more interested in sending their antiterrorist unit to the scene than setting up roadblocks. The enemy did encounter a roadblock, but it wasn't well prepared or well armed. The terrorists shot their way through and kept going. The two cars and truck used to flee the area were later found abandoned. They must have swapped vehicles to get out of the city."

"You're sure they got away? Maybe the army or the *federales* will cut them off before they can retreat to the jungle."

"Probably would have heard news on their capture by now," the warrior replied. "There's still a chance the authorities might find the terrorists, but I wouldn't hold my breath in anticipation. The Indian rebels have been pretty good at avoiding military patrols in the past, and Valdez recruited most of his personnel from their ranks. We'd better assume he and his comrades got away."

Brognola frowned. "You sound certain Valdez is still out there. They haven't identified all the dead terrorists and you said several of them were badly burned and mutilated by explosions and fires during the battle. Maybe he was taken out and they're still scraping him off the pavement."

"Maybe," Bolan allowed, "but I doubt it. The guy is a survivor. He probably hauled ass in time to avoid being taken out by the pipe-bomb missile. Valdez was wounded—not seriously, but enough to reduce his ability to fight. He'd know the best course of action would be to retreat after the bomb exploded and sirens warned reinforcements were on their way. My guess is he was one of the first to reach a vehicle to flee the area. It was the only logical move to make under the circumstances."

"Well, the good guys won this round. Valdez lost a lot of people in the firefight. This was sort of his big chance to save face and his own followers might turn on him now.''

''Hard to say what might happen. We can spin any sort of conjecture we want, but we can't count on somebody else doing us a favor by taking care of Valdez for whatever reason. Better we assume he's still at large and doesn't intend to retire from the terrorist business.''

''You're probably right,'' Brognola admitted. ''I just wish I could pass on something more definite to the President. This isn't the only problem the Man in the Oval Office has on his plate. You're probably not getting much news about what's going on here in the States. The President is under fire by critics for failure to deliver on certain campaign promises, they're racking up some more rumors of misconduct and it looks like he might have another scandal to deal with.''

''That's his problem. Comes with the job and he knew it. He worked hard enough to get in the White House, and now he has to take everything that comes with the office.''

''Yeah,'' Brognola agreed. ''Still, the President is under a lot of pressure and he's looking for us to give him some favorable news to prove his administration is doing something right. I know—before you say it— we're not part of his administration. Stony Man was in operation before he took office and we'll probably be here after he's gone, but the general public doesn't know we exist and we have to keep it that way. Fact is, we need the President's cooperation to function efficiently with a low profile.''

"Well, this mission could have gone smoother if we'd had a little cooperation. CIA never did deliver that M-16 with an M-203 launcher and the additional grenades and explosives requested for this mission. I've been forced to improvise in the field more than I should have, Hal."

"We'll take care of that supply snag."

"I've already taken care of that. This time I helped myself to what was left on the battlefield by the dead and retreating enemy. The terrorists had plenty of assault weapons and explosives, and they left a small arsenal on the streets."

"Valdez was an arms dealer. I guess he was able to get just about anything he wanted for his personal army. The point I was trying to make, Striker, is the President wants results. You and I know this was a victory over the terrorists. The news reports will say Marine security forces and the local police protected the embassy and the ambassador from a terrorist attack. They'll give the body count on both sides and officially praise the forces that stopped the enemy. But this incident is still going to scare the hell out of a lot of U.S. investors and businesses that plan to participate in the North American Free Trade Agreement."

"It was said that would happen after Colosio was assassinated," Bolan remarked. "He was a leading supporter of NAFTA here in Mexico. I don't think that frightened many U.S. companies from participation."

"But Valdez has deliberately targeted U.S. companies and institutions," the big Fed insisted. "That's why you're there, Striker. Wouldn't have asked you to go if this wasn't a direct threat to American interests and American lives. I also know I don't have to tell you that."

"And I don't have to tell you I'm not an economics expert. I don't know if NAFTA is more positive or negative for the people of the United States or Mexico. I'm not here to defend it. I'm here to save lives and stop terrorism. If the President wants something to improve his image, tell him to consult his public relations advisers."

"Look, Striker," Brognola began, "I have to make a progress report to the Man. I'm not a bullshit artist either. I'd like to tell the President this whole mess is over, but I'm not going to lie to him. Enough people do that already. What I can tell him is the terrorists suffered a major ass-kicking, and their number has been chopped down dramatically. We figure Valdez can't have more than a hundred to a hundred and fifty followers. Don't guess more than that number would throw in with such an extremist."

"So I've only got to worry about between forty to eighty-some terrorists," Bolan said dryly. "Hate to tell you this, Hal, but that's more than enough."

"I realize that, but I can still tell the President the terrorist forces have been cut by half and the leader may or may not be dead. The mission isn't over yet, but your progress has been outstanding and the enemy is pretty much broken and on the run."

"Okay. Just don't believe things are quite that sunny. The terrorists will probably head back to the jungle to lick their wounds and consider what to do next. Don't count on their giving up. Fanatics seldom do. I doubt Valdez and his people will launch another hasty attack after what happened. They'll take their time, recover from this loss as best they can and try to pick a new target that seems safer.''

''Any idea what that might be?''

''Not really. The only other site we knew the terrorists planned to attack was the U.S. auto plant to the north. They may be reluctant to go for it now. More likely they'll choose a smaller, easier target. Maybe hunt for some more visiting VIPs from the United States. Maybe even settle for killing some regular American tourists.''

''Can't provide protection for everybody who might wind up on their hit list,'' Brognola commented. ''If you knew where to find the bastards you might go after them and nail the rats in their nest, but the Mexican government hasn't had much luck so it's not likely you can locate the terrorist base. Is it?''

''Maybe with some help from you folks back at the Farm. More than thirty terrorists participated in the attack on the embassy. That many people moving through the rain forest and emerging somewhere along the jungle limits to get the vehicles needed for the trip to Mexico City could have been observed by surveillance satellites in orbit over the Yucatán and south central portion of Mexico. We have access to information from NSA Signal Intelligence satellites and similar high-tech spies in the sky used by CIA, Office of Naval Intelligence and whoever else has those su-

persnoop devices spinning around the world. Maybe
the Bear can work some computer magic and come up
with some information. If we know where the terrorists came from, it'll help us find where they are now."

"Worth a try," the big Fed agreed. "I'll get Aaron
on it immediately. How about your contacts in Mexico? Santos was your main man and he's dead. How
well connected is the guy's sister?"

"She seems to have pretty reliable sources within the
police and federal outfits," Bolan replied, "but I don't
want to push her if I don't have to. Ellena and her
brother were close. She's taking this loss pretty hard.
Ramon and Raul are helping me now. They have connections, mostly through their late cousin, and they
handled themselves pretty well in that firefight. So did
Karl Brunjes."

"He's a desk jockey, not a field agent."

"All the more reason to praise the way he handled
himself. The ambassador might have been killed before I could reach the embassy if Karl hadn't been alert
to danger and got the man to cover. I'm not too
thrilled with the CIA in general right now, but Karl
deserves a good word to somebody in a high place in
the Company."

"I hear you. Brunjes will probably get more cooperation from the CIA and the Mexican authorities
since your prediction about the attack on the embassy
proved accurate and most will see Brunjes as the guy
who gave the warning."

"I don't care who gets the credit as long as we can get the job done here," the Executioner replied. "That about wraps it up for now, Hal."

"Right. Watch your tail, buddy."

Bolan signed off.

ADOLFO VALDEZ DREW the pencil across a sketch paper. The ache in his forearm protested, but he ignored the pain. Three buckshot pellets had been pried from the limb. No major veins or arteries had been struck, and the tearing to muscles was minimal. There would be scars, of course, but Valdez didn't care. He already carried dozens of scars as tattoos of surviving violence. The real scars left by the battle at the embassy were deep within his mind.

The raid had been a failure. Only Valdez and eight of his followers managed to escape alive. Two had been seriously wounded and would probably die from internal bleeding. It was the most bitter defeat Valdez had ever experienced because he had personally planned the assault. Someone else had anticipated his tactics to outthink and outfight his forces.

Valdez drew the tall, athletic figure from memory. He had natural artistic ability, although it had never been formally trained. He sketched the khaki trousers and open field jacket with little detail to wrinkles and folds of fabric. The clothes didn't matter. The man who wore them was his only interest. He had glimpsed the warrior's face. Strong features, a stern mouth and determined eyes. Valdez couldn't guess the man's ethnic background by his appearance, yet he had no doubt the mystery soldier was an experienced combat veteran.

How old was he? Valdez wondered. Hard to determine. Late thirties, perhaps early to mid-forties. He could have been in Vietnam. Probably a former member of an elite military unit. Special Forces, Airborne Ranger, Navy SEAL, something like that. Training similar to Valdez himself and more experience to develop his skills. The man's strategy was impressive; he was certainly good with weapons and still moved well. Survival instincts obviously remained at peak level with this warhorse.

Valdez wished he could meet the man in a one-to-one fight. His youth would be in his favor. The years weigh heavily on a man's speed and stamina. If Valdez could fight him close quarters, with cold steel or bare hands... then he would see how good this warrior really was. Valdez had to admire his opponent, yet he would find great satisfaction in breaking the man's neck or cutting him to ribbons.

"What are you doing?" a voice asked in Spanish from the mouth of Valdez's tent.

Hector Arguello entered. He glanced at the sketch and frowned. Valdez set it down and rose from his cot.

"Who are you drawing a picture of? Another proposed target for assassination? If it is supposed to be the gringo vice president, it's not a very good likeness. I doubt he'll be making any trips to Mexico for a while. Or do you plan to head north of the border to hunt him down in Washington?"

"I saw him at the embassy," Valdez explained. "He's the man who did this to my arm and killed several of our comrades. I'm sure he's the same man I saw on the hill that night at the auto-repair shop. I know, Hector. I only saw him briefly on each occasion, but I'm certain of this. He's some kind of combat expert. A fighting machine and a commander...."

"This man is not important. He's just one person. We have the entire governments of Mexico and the United States to deal with. You're thinking of this as some sort of personal matter between yourself and this man. It is not. We are fighting for a cause and all our lives are on the line if we fail."

Valdez looked at Arguello. The small, soft-faced nerdish character had a lot of nerve to talk to him in such a manner. Yet Valdez respected Arguello and knew he had a point.

"You're right, my friend," he admitted. "We've had our biggest defeat since we started this private war. How do we recover from it? What do you suggest we do now?"

"Take inventory of our losses and replace them," the senior man replied. "Obviously we lost a lot of our people. Don't think about building up the ranks just yet. We can always recruit more followers from the disgruntled masses. Give them a reason to believe in you and they'll flock to join us."

"If you're not talking about the lives we've lost, what losses are you talking about?"

"That's obvious. We lost all but four of our vehicles in Mexico City. Of course, we can steal some cars and trucks, but getting vehicles in good condition with powerful engines and reliable tires isn't so easy. You took a great deal of firepower to that embassy assault. Not much came back. We still have enough assault rifles and submachine guns for most of the forces here at the base, but not enough to offer such modern weapons to new members. We have only two grenade launchers left, we're short on hand grenades and eventually we'll run low on ammunition for the weapons as well.''

"You have been busy taking inventory," Valdez remarked.

"Check for yourself if you think I'm wrong. The fact is, Adolfo, rebels came to you because you offered something the Zapatistas did not. You were willing to take a more offensive action against the government and the Americans, but you could back that up with military expertise and better supplies and weapons for your troops. Now, they'll doubt your ability to carry off successful missions after the embassy defeat, and you're running out of the supplies and hardware as well. If you're going to continue to lead these people, you have to do something about that and soon."

"I don't have a large supply of weapons anymore," Valdez said. "I had them smuggled here before I moved from the States. I don't have any money, either. All my savings went into this project. The cash in our treasury is all that's left."

"I appreciate that," Arguello replied. "You put everything you had into this, but it isn't enough. We have to get more weapons and supplies. That means we need more money. For that matter, we should get some sort of pay to our troops if you want to keep morale high.''

''They're freedom fighters, not mercenaries. They didn't join us to make a profit.''

''You were a soldier. You didn't enlist in the United States Army to make money. You had patriotic reasons when you joined, but you still expected to get paid every month. Our people have left families, friends and familiar settings to join our cause. They need all the encouragement and promises of future comfort we can give them. Some money in their pockets will make them feel better.''

''They don't need money here, Hector. We're in a fucking jungle. What the hell would they do with money here?''

''Dedication to a cause is based on belief and attitude, not logic. Anything that helps them believe in you and improve their attitude will be in your favor.''

''What you're saying is we need money. I thought you regarded capitalism and materialism with contempt. Your former Communist comrades would be very disappointed in you, Hector.''

''Communism is dead,'' Arguello said dryly. ''Haven't you heard that before? Besides, we needed capital to operate when I was with the 23rd September Movement. Our outfit had similar problems back then to what we're having now. Be it the root of all evil or not, we need money.''

''Do you have any idea how we can get some?''

"Same way the 23rd September used to get it," Arguello replied. "We go where they keep money and take some. We need to rob some banks. Unless you can think of some other source that will allow us to get cash in a hurry."

"We could kidnap someone and hold the person for ransom. Perhaps some rich American."

"That will take time to arrange payments under circumstances that will allow us to get the money without being captured. Robbing banks takes less time."

"It's also more difficult than when you and your Commie comrades used to do it almost twenty years ago," Valdez warned. "They don't keep as much cash by the tellers these days and they've improved communications with the police, silent alarms and computers and all the other high-tech pain-in-the-ass problems bank robbers face these days."

"So we won't get as much money as we used to in the past. The process will be simple enough. Go in, tell them to give us the money, grab what we can and run like hell. Bank security in this country is less sophisticated than in the United States."

"It still seems like a lot of risk for a fairly low amount of profit. There might be more potential for larger sums of cash by robbing a pharmacy or even a supermarket."

"I'm not sure about that," Arguello replied, "but I am sure they still have money in banks. That much hasn't changed. Let me handle this. I've done enough bank robberies in the past, and the authorities will be looking for you. Your cover is burned and the Feds, police and this gringo bastard you were drawing all know about you. I'm old news and I look harmless. My odds are much better for this sort of mission."

"I suppose you're right, Hector."

"We have some people who have participated in robberies before. Let me take four or five of them. Not hotheads. We don't want any shooting unless necessary. I'll also need at least one vehicle and a good driver."

"You'll have the best we can offer, Hector," Valdez assured him. "Just be careful. I've got enough problems without losing my chief adviser."

"Don't worry about me," the older man replied. He pointed at the sketch and added, "Try not to worry about that man, either."

Valdez glanced at the drawing and frowned.

"Whoever he is, I'm sure he's thinking about me and we haven't seen the last of him."

8

Jack Grimaldi walked down the ramp to Gate 43 at the international airport in Mexico City. He smiled when he saw Mack Bolan accompanied by two men who looked remarkably alike. Grimaldi shook hands with the warrior, who briefly introduced him to Ramon and Raul.

"I guessed you guys might be the twin brothers they told me about," Grimaldi remarked. "By the way, my passport has the name Jake Grissim. Try to remember it. I'm having enough trouble because they gave me the cover ID in a hurry."

"I know," Bolan replied. "Hardly got word about your arrival in time to meet your flight. Let's get your luggage, Mr. Grissim."

They moved into the droves of passenger-arrivals headed for the customs and baggage area. Relatively few visitors from the United States had been on board Grimaldi's flight. Reports of terrorist attacks on U.S. citizens had clearly scared away much of the tourism to Mexico City.

The Executioner noticed airport security had increased, but the concern appeared centered on possible sabotage attacks rather than smugglers entering the country. Many North Americans think of Mexico as a place things are smuggled from, not into. Yet smuggling is a major problem in Mexico. Drugs are smuggled in from other Central American and South American countries, often en route to the United States. Firearms and money—the latter illegally gained profits or cash to be used for illegal purposes—shuffle into Mexico from both north and south.

The publicity and politics involved in the recent wave of terrorism had changed security practices—at least temporarily. Valdez wouldn't attempt an attack on the airport. Bolan felt certain of that. But he didn't know what target would be next or how much longer until the terrorists decided to launch another attack.

Grimaldi finished with customs, then joined Bolan and the twins. They said little as they left the airport and walked to the van parked in the visitors' section. They loaded Grimaldi's suitcase in the back and climbed into the rig. Raul started the engine and soon the vehicle rolled from the lot into a stream of dense traffic.

"Mike tells us you're a pilot, Mr. Grissim," Ramon said. "If you plan to search the jungle from the air to try to locate the terrorist base, you must know the military has tried that many times before."

"Yeah," Grimaldi replied. "I know. We're hoping we might be able to get some additional information that might help from the satellite surveillance reports. Besides, you never know when you might need an air taxi service or maybe some firepower from the sky."

"We've worked together before," Bolan stated. "Jake is the best combat pilot I've ever known."

The Executioner and Grimaldi went back a long way. They had participated in missions during Bolan's former campaigns against the Mob, and the Stony Man pilot had spent a while working on the wrong side of the law before he met Bolan. The warrior was glad to have Grimaldi aboard if only for moral support.

"By the way," Grimaldi began, "the boss said he's sorry he couldn't send the Three Musketeers as well, but they're tied up with a project at home."

Bolan nodded. The pilot referred to Able Team, a trio of veteran fighting men and comrades in arms of the Executioner's.

"Can't have everything to make life easier," Bolan commented, "but we can count on cooperation from the authorities through Karl at the embassy. After we beat back the terrorists the last time, the *federales* and other Mexican officials are willing to help any way they can."

"That's because we got results when no one else could," Raul stated.

"Can't argue with success," Grimaldi said. "How about the Company? Are they still lying down on the job with supplies?"

"Karl is their golden boy now," Bolan replied. "I don't think you'll have any trouble getting any high-tech gear for a chopper. Heat sensors, night vision, advanced radar and whatever else you think will work in the whirlybird you'll be using."

"Where do I get the chopper? 'Helicopters 'R Us'?"

"The Mexican army will provide it," Bolan answered. "The best choice seemed to be a Bell gunship. I know you're familiar with the model."

"You bet," Grimaldi said. "I'll want to do some work on it myself and take the bird up for a test flight before taking it into the field. If there's anything wrong with the chopper or the other gear, I want to know about it in advance so I can fix it before I fly into a combat zone."

"We'll give you everything you need," Bolan assured him. "Hopefully that will include the time you need to make sure all the equipment is in top condition. That will depend on what the terrorists do. They're not working on our timetable."

"Has there been any more terrorist activity since the embassy shoot-out?" Grimaldi asked.

"Not yet," Bolan answered. "The military and the *federales* searched the city and the surrounding area. They set up roadblocks, but the terrorists must have already ditched their vehicles. Nobody is sure how they managed to escape, but they did it. Valdez wasn't among the dead at the embassy and I'm sure he wasn't mortally wounded in the firefight. The guy's still out there. He's not going to quit. We just don't know how much longer the enemy will remain in hiding or what they might try next."

"It'd be nice if we could locate the sons of bitches and nail them before they can cause any more grief," the pilot remarked.

"Yeah," the Executioner agreed. "That would be nice."

THE VAN ROLLED to the reserved parking area behind the twins' hardware store. They continued to use the place for a safehouse because it was close to the U.S. embassy, the Mexico City police headquarters and the Internal Security Division at the capital. Raul parked the vehicle and they headed for the building. Ellena Santos opened the door to meet them at the threshold.

She appeared tired, grim and unhappy. Bolan hadn't expected to see her at the safehouse. Ellena acknowledged him with a weary nod. The death of her brother had obviously left the woman physically and emotionally exhausted.

"We thought you would be spending today preparing for...for Miguel," Ramon remarked.

"The funeral is tomorrow," she replied. "There's nothing more I can do for now except continue his work. When this is over I'll decide what to do in the future, but this is unfinished business that must be ended before my brother can truly rest in peace."

Bolan nodded. "We can use your help. You still have contacts with the authorities we don't have."

"And I've been in touch with them," she stated as she opened her large handbag. "We might have a possible lead. A bank in Veracruz was robbed this morning. The thieves shot a security guard and two tellers. They successfully escaped with twenty thousand pesos."

She removed several photographs from the bag and explained they were still shots from the bank's surveillance cameras. A close-up featured a round-faced man with dark glasses and a cloth cap.

"A special investigator for the Criminal Investigation Division thought he recognized this man among the bank robbers," Ellena explained. "He was clearly the leader of the group. We ran a computer check on known felons with a history of bank robbery who are still at large. One name emerged as fitting the general description of this man, if one added an extra fifteen years or so to his face and body."

She reached into the bag again for a photocopy of a criminal file on Hector Arguello. "Arguello is now in his early forties. Twenty years ago he was an angry young man with the left-wing 23rd September Movement. I'm sure you've heard of it."

"I thought they were washed up," Grimaldi commented. "Pretty much died out when international communism was on its last unsteady, dying legs."

"Yes," Ellena replied, "but not all the members of the 23rd September were captured or killed. Some remain at large, and many committed crimes they have yet to pay for. Arguello was involved in a number of such actions. He is still wanted for attempted treason and trying to overthrow the Republic of Mexico by force and violence, murder, conspiracy to commit murder, kidnapping and several charges of armed robbery. These include bank robberies, apparently to raise money for the Movement at the time."

"So it's possible this guy has joined Valdez and resorted to his old ways of getting a big bank loan with a gun," Bolan commented. "Valdez isn't a Communist, but Arguello is probably disillusioned with his old politics by now and willing to join any outfit that will take him. Valdez is certainly smart enough to realize a veteran terrorist and long-time survivor like Arguello would be a useful ally. Anybody who can avoid getting caught for more than two decades must have some good advice for others to do likewise."

"Yes," Ramon agreed. "Perhaps. Or perhaps this bank robbery has nothing to do with Valdez. Arguello might be acting on his own. Perhaps he even took advantage of the fact the forces of law enforcement are now busy with different terrorists so he figured he could pull a bank job—like you Americans would say—and get away with it."

"Let's assume for a moment there is a connection," Bolan suggested. "Everybody agrees Valdez doesn't have a huge following. He's probably lost at least half his people and a fair amount of weaponry. We also suspect he pretty much financed this operation on his own. That means he may be short on personnel, short on weapons and short on cash."

"Emphasis on the latter," Grimaldi added. "If he can get enough money, he can buy more guns and attract more recruits."

"Even if you're right," Raul began, "I don't understand why this would help us find the terrorists. Do you think they'll try to rob more banks?"

"How much is twenty thousand pesos in American money?" Grimaldi asked.

"Less than ten dollars," Ellena replied.

"Jesus," the pilot muttered. "They killed those people for a lousy ten bucks?"

"Bad luck for Arguello as well as the people they murdered," Bolan replied. "Obviously he'll have to rob some more banks or get more money somehow. We can't cover all the banks throughout Mexico, but maybe we can figure which target might have the most appeal to the terrorists."

"You don't think they'd go after the federal reserves at our treasury?" Ramon asked in an astonished tone. "That would be insane. It's surrounded by troops and has very tight security."

"I doubt it," Bolan assured him. "They'll look for something that involves considerably less risk, but still has a high profit level."

"Mexico is an oil-producing nation," Grimaldi commented. "The petroleum business here must earn a fortune, and they must deposit at least part of that profit in banks somewhere."

"I believe most of the oil profits are transferred to cashier checks," Ramon stated. "We know our currency is ranked low in value compared to the United States. Mexico has always had high inflation and every major corporation here knows this. They tend to put profits into cashier checks for security reasons or directly invest in stocks, bonds or commodities."

"You said Arguello is also wanted for kidnapping," Bolan said to Ellena. "Maybe they'll turn to that method to raise funds through ransom. There are also money exchange posts throughout the country that change foreign currency to Mexican pesos and cash checks. Obviously they have to have a lot of money on hand... probably in American dollars as well as Mexican currency.''

''Yeah,'' Grimaldi said. ''I'm sure if we thought about it hard enough we could come up with a thousand possible targets for the terrorists and still not guess the right one. How the hell could we cover every maybe on the list? We'd have to get every cop, local and federal, in the country to help stake out all of them.''

''Still,'' the Executioner stated, ''we need to alert the authorities to the possibility of these terrorist actions. Maybe they can't cover everything, but they might get lucky and nail Arguello in the act. Might save some lives too. You take care of that while I go upstairs for a little privacy while I call Hal.''

''Well,'' Grimaldi said, ''I hate to feel like I'm wasting my time and there's not much I can do here. Your friend at the embassy ought to have a package for me and I'd like to start work on that helicopter as soon as possible.''

''Sure. Ramon or Raul can drive you over to see Karl and then on to the hangar where your new chopper is waiting.''

Bolan turned to Ellena and added, ''Good work. I think you might have found a solid lead for us.''

She almost smiled and said, ''We'll see.''

BOLAN BRIEFED Brognola on what had occurred since Grimaldi's arrival. The big Fed braced his elbows on the conference table and rested his chin on his fists as he considered the possible connection between the Arguello bank robbery and Valdez's terrorist outfit.

"Sounds like this guy really screwed up," Brognola remarked. "If he plans to use the money from that bank job to buy weapons and finance terrorism, he'll be lucky to pick up a decent bowie knife."

"Don't underestimate Arguello because he made a poor choice for a robbery," Bolan said. "It must have been a long time since he robbed a bank, and he didn't really appreciate how little cash the tellers would have in their drawers. He won't make that same mistake again. The guy hasn't been winning hide-and-seek with the police and *federales* because he's stupid."

"Okay. Let's assume you're right. You don't know where he's going to hit next. Sure you can contact the police and federal outfits, but Arguello could knock over half a dozen places before the law-enforcement agencies figure out how they want to provide protection."

"Maybe they'll get lucky," Bolan replied. "I'm not counting on that. What I think we should concentrate on is the possibility the terrorists will try to buy arms from Valdez's cronies in the States. When he gets enough money together for a deal, it seems likely he'll go to his gunrunning associates to make the buy."

"You got a point, Striker," Brognola agreed. "We'll get a list of Valdez's known associates and see about getting wiretaps on their phones and surveillance on them as fast as possible.''

''There's a chance Valdez may try to contact them by shortwave radio rather than telephone. Need to run radio frequency scans in case they attempt that form of communication.''

''We're still working on gathering and processing data from the spy satellites. Now, of course, we'll have to add searching for evidence of Arguello and his band of bank-robbing bandits to the list.''

Bolan heard someone on the stairs. He turned to the doorway and saw Ellena approach the threshold. She saw the warrior seated by the telephone and stopped by the entrance.

''Sorry to disturb you,'' she said, ''but I just spoke with that CID investigator on the phone. He tells me another robbery occurred only a few minutes ago. Apparently it was Arguello and his group. This time they struck at Acapulco. No one was prepared for it because they did not expect the terrorists to hit another target so far away so quickly.''

''Was it another bank?'' Bolan asked.

''One of the major luxury hotels that caters to wealthy visitors. The thieves caught the hotel security people completely off guard. No one expected anything so daring in broad daylight. They forced the staff to open the vaults and took nearly all the cash and jewelry. They're not certain exactly how much was stolen, but the hotel manager estimates it was approximately two million dollars, including the value of the jewelry.''

"Two million dollars," Bolan repeated into the mouthpiece. "I'd say Valdez has enough to buy more than a bowie knife."

"We'll get those warrants ready as fast as possible," Brognola replied.

"I sure hope so," the Executioner replied, "because it's obvious the other side isn't wasting any time."

9

Garrett Farrel hadn't expected to hear from Al Valdez. He was less than pleased to discover the renegade had left a message on the answering machine of his home phone. At least the son of a bitch hadn't left his real name, but he had left a telephone number with an area code in Mexico. The Feds frequently had Farrel's phone tapped and they knew Valdez had boogied south of the border.

He wondered, once again, if Valdez had anything to do with all the terrorist crap in Mexico that had been reported on the news since the guy left the States. Farrel had been partners with Valdez for almost two years, but they had never really become friends. Valdez didn't like Anglos, and Farrel didn't care much for Hispanics. Too emotional to be good businessmen, Farrel figured. Too worried about proving their machismo and trying to get even with everybody who ever pissed them off. Farrel believed time spent trying to get revenge was time lost from trying to make money.

They had made some money for a while. Farrel couldn't complain about Valdez's willingness to take risks by trekking to Mexico and other Latin American countries to make deals with would-be revolutionaries, cocaine syndicates and other crazies no one in his or her right mind would want to go near. So Valdez was a little nuts. Maybe that was why he was good at handling business with other Hispanic lunatics. Farrel could supply the guns, explosives and ammunition, but he needed reliable people to help him distribute and sell the hardware to customers willing to pay for his goods.

Everybody wanted guns, and Farrel made a fortune in the black market arms trade. He had one of the most successful gunrunning rackets in Florida. Farrel got weapons right off the assembly line from gun manufacturers. He knew importers who smuggled in a few extra firearms for extra profit. Crooked cops in five cities lifted guns from the confiscated weapons rooms to sell to Farrel, which were officially "destroyed." Farrel specialized in military hardware. Not the so-called "semiautomatic assault weapons" the politicians whined about banning from the general public. Farrel handled the real thing—full-auto rifles and submachine guns. He even supplied rocket launchers, M-60 machine guns and .50-caliber tank mounts from time to time. To put his supply out of business they would have to stop producing such weapons for the armed forces of the United States of America. There would always be buyers. Farrel could get an illegal gun for five hundred dollars and sell it the same day for two thousand.

Business was always good for Garrett Farrel, but like most people, he was better at recognizing the flaws in others than dealing with his own problems. He was too fond of expensive cars, expensive women and expensive drugs, and he had spent hundreds of thousands of dollars satisfying those appetites. Add that to the expense of his business—hiring personnel to get the goods and distribute them, transportation costs and lawyer fees to keep him out of prison—and there wasn't much left over.

Sure, Farrel lived in a fancy, art deco-style house in a Miami suburb, but he was two months late on his rent because he'd spent too much on feeding his nose cocaine. He knew he'd never own that house if he kept missing payments, and he also needed to build a nest egg for the future. He was good at making money, even better at spending it, but Farrel had never been good at saving a dime. He figured if he got a big score, a really big score, he'd put it aside for his retirement. Sooner or later he'd have to quit the gunrunning business. Farrel had been lucky and he'd never served any hard time, but nobody's luck lasted forever. The Feds and the local police knew what he was doing, but they hadn't been able to prove it.

Farrel thought about these matters as he drove his sleek black Mercedes to the Royal Blue Restaurant. It was his favorite spot for lunch and afternoon cocktails, and possessed a pay phone inside a secure booth of wood and glass. The arms dealer didn't intend to try to call Valdez from his home phone. He was reluctant to contact the man at all, but Valdez wouldn't have left the message unless he wanted to buy more arms, and this could be the big score Farrel was looking for.

He parked his car, entered the restaurant and headed for the call box. The arms dealer took an address book from his jacket pocket and removed a small piece of paper. He unfolded it to read the message copied from the answering machine. Valdez had referred to himself as "Vic Sharp" and said he had called Farrel after speaking with "Jason." These were code expressions Farrel used for business in case the Feds had his phone tapped. "Sharp" meant Farrel's pocket calculator made by the Sharp Corporation. The numbers on this calculator—and the majority of others—were set in a square shape, three buttons across and three down. The top horizontal line read 7-8-9, the second line 4-5-6 and the last 1-2-3.

The phone number Valdez left was meant to be decoded using the calculator to unscramble the order of the numbers. The number one meant the first number on the Sharp calculator—seven. Two would be eight, three equalled nine and so on to nine, which meant three. Only zero remained the same.

"Jason" referred to the hockey-mask killer from the *Friday the 13th* horror films. Farrel was a movie buff. The "Jason" code meant "thirteen." In this case, it meant 1300 hours or one o'clock in the afternoon. Valdez had better know about any time differences, Farrel thought as he consulted his watch, because he was calling at one o'clock Miami time, not whatever the hell it might be in Mexico.

He peeled open a roll of quarters and fed ten dollars in coins into the phone. It rang once at the other end of the line and a voice answered immediately.

"This is Vic Sharp."

"Hi, Vic," Farrel replied. "How do you like Mexico?"

"I've been busy," Valdez stated.

"Anything I might have heard about?"

"Do you really want to know?"

"No," Farrel admitted, "I don't think so. Just tell me what you want from me. Don't expect any favors, Vic. You're just another customer now."

"I realize that," Valdez assured him. "I need the usual. The best you can get and as soon as possible. At least two hundred rifles, a hundred and fifty submachine guns and machine pistols, twenty or thirty mounted machine guns and at least that many rocket and grenade launchers. Of course we'll need ammunition for all the weapons, as well as about five hundred M-26 hand grenades and twenty kilos of C-4. I'd like the first delivery made in two days—"

"Hold on, Vic. I'm still writing this down. I don't know goddamn shorthand. You're talking a shitload of hardware, pal. It's going to be expensive. If you're serious about all this, it'll run at least eight hundred or nine hundred thousand dollars."

"You could do it for a bit less than that," Valdez remarked. "We both know that, but I expected the bill to be about that amount. The first payment on the first delivery will be four hundred and fifty thousand dollars. Hell, we'll make it five hundred thousand. Is that fair enough?"

Farrel bit his tongue. He didn't want to sound too eager. This could be the big score he'd been looking for, but he didn't want Valdez to know how hot he was for the deal.

"You have that kind of cash on hand, Vic?"

"More than that," Valdez assured him. "If all goes well with the shipments and we're happy with the merchandise, you can expect some more big orders from us in the future."

"Okay. I think we've got a deal."

Farrel pawed at his nose. He could use some blow. Hell, he had a big score in the works with more to come. He figured he could afford to see his favorite coke dealer to pick up some nose candy. Tonight, Farrel thought, he'd party hardy. Women and drugs and good times. Plenty of money would be rolling in now, and he could save enough for retirement and still enjoy some of his vices.

Couldn't he?

LEO TURRIN PULLED into the parking lot of the Royal Blue and stopped his Honda rental next to the big black Mercedes. He gathered up the handset to a special federal police-band radio unit and punched a button that served as a redial. A beep sounded in his ear, followed by the voice of Justice Department Agent Roger Duvall.

"Yeah," Turrin announced. "I'm here waiting for Mr. Wonderful. Seems to be taking his time having lunch. Probably knocked back a few cocktails and hit on the waitresses. Hope he doesn't spend all day in there."

"We're on our way to back you up, Mr. Justice," Duvall declared. "Shouldn't try to take him by yourself."

"Don't worry about me," Turrin replied. "You guys check that tape to make sure everything came out okay? Hate to have evidence that won't stand up because there's too much static or it's missing vital details."

"Clear as a bell," the agent assured him. "We got him, sir."

Turrin remembered the man who stepped from the restaurant from computer printout photos at Stony Man Farm. Farrel appeared slightly heavier than in the pictures, and his face was more puffy around the eyes and jowls. The sun seemed to catch Farrel off guard. He staggered on unsteady legs and fumbled for a pair of gold-frame shades.

"Correction," Turrin declared. "I got him right here. I'm going to say hello before he can get in his Mercedes."

"We'll be there in a few minutes."

"Great," Turrin replied. "See you when you get here."

He hung up the handset before Duvall could protest. The little Fed reached inside his jacket as he opened the car door with his other hand, drawing a snubnose .38 Smith & Wesson from leather as he emerged from the Honda. Turrin dropped his arm to his side to hide the gun behind his thigh. He shuffled to the rear of the car and smiled at Farrel as the gunrunner approached.

Farrel weaved in midstride and stared at Turrin. He had consumed a few drinks and his judgment was affected, but he knew something was wrong. This little guy in a cheap suit with a flashy necktie looked like he was either a hood with poor taste or a cop. Either way, it meant trouble. Turrin ended the suspense by flashing an ID card with a gold badge.

"This thing says I'm Leo Justice with the Department of Justice. Need to talk to you, Farrel. Got five to twenty years to spare?"

Farrel held his arms apart, hands low, but open with the palms up. He guessed this so-called Fed had a weapon hidden from view, and he wanted to make it clear he wasn't armed.

"Your name is Justice and you're with the Justice Department?" he asked. "Expect me to buy that crap?"

Turrin tossed the ID folder on the trunk of the Honda.

"You come here and take a better look at that," he invited. "While you're at it, put your hands on the car and assume the position. Don't screw around, Farrel. You know what I'm talking about."

The arms dealer cursed under his breath, but obeyed instructions. He placed his palms on the Honda and spread his legs. Turrin got out a pair of steel handcuffs.

"You going to arrest me, pig, or is this just some harassment? I have a lawsuit in progress against the FBI and the BATF for unconstitutional harassment. Guess it's time to do the same with you assholes."

"Well, you are under arrest. Don't worry. I'll read you your rights after I frisk you and put the cuffs on you."

"What the hell is the charge—?"

Farrel started to turn as he spoke and raised his hands from the car. Turrin swung up the .38 and let the guy see it. The arms dealer put his hands back on the Honda.

"We got a bunch of charges for you, pal. You're selling illegal arms and explosives, you're aiding and abetting an international terrorist and that makes you an accessory to his crimes as well. That includes murder, treason and conspiracy."

"I don't know what you're talking about, but I want my lawyer. You don't have nothin' on me."

"I'm going to have these cuffs on you in a minute," Turrin replied. "We also have a tape of your conversation with one Adolfo Valdez. You talked to him less than two hours ago on the phone inside this establishment."

"You don't have a tape of any conversation."

"Don't be stupid," Turrin said. "We had a wiretap on the pay phone at the Royal Blue as well as half a dozen other public telephones at places you like to hang out. We got permission from federal judges for the wiretaps and it's all legal. No violation of Fourth Amendment rights as long as we use only information from a conversation that you had while talking on that public phone. Might have trouble nailing anybody else who was making dope deals, arranging for hit men or threatening to kill the President, but we were only after you anyway, and we damn well got you.''

Farrel clenched his fists, but kept them on the hood of the car. He wasn't a tough guy, and he knew it. The arms dealer shook his head to clear cobwebs caused by alcohol.

"Wait a minute," he began. "You went to too much trouble just to go after me. Valdez is the one you really want. That's what this is all about, right?"

"Maybe so," Turrin replied, "but we got you right now."

"Hey," Farrel said. "I'll help you get Valdez. We can make a deal. What do you say?"

"I say I'm not so sure you have anything to make a deal with," Turrin stated. "I don't know that you have anything to add to what we already have on tape concerning Valdez's activities, but if you want to talk we'll listen. Of course, you do have a right to remain silent and if you give up that right anything you say can and will be used against you in a court of law...."

10

Mack Bolan adjusted the Starlight goggles as he scanned the pier. It was a neglected, lonely spot located between the coastal city of Alvarado and the Bay of Campeche. The pier had never been a major port, although it had once been the site of limited business for pleasure boating and fishing. An oil tanker had spilled several thousand gallons of black crude in the waters, and much of it had floated into the harbor area. Too small to attract much interest from the government or international ecology organizations, the oil slick was all but ignored.

A small wooden shop with a tar paper roof and a toolshed still stood by the plank walk, but the former business there had been closed for more than a year. The rotted hull of a wooden rowboat lay discarded, never to be repaired or used again. A sign written in Spanish and English warned the waters were polluted and prohibited fishing or swimming. The little harbor was useless for anyone except smugglers.

Valdez had previously learned about the pier when he was still Garrett Farrel's partner. It proved to be an ideal spot for illegal arms deliveries, unnoticed by the authorities or coastal patrols. The gunrunners had successfully used the simple tactic of using boats headed for ports at Veracruz, Alvarado or the Bay of Campeche. The vessels apparently wandered off course to make covert transactions with the clients. The oil slick jammed by the pier even helped them locate the area.

The Executioner learned this information from Hal Brognola after the arrest and interrogation of Garrett Farrel in Miami. The arms dealer had told the Feds everything he knew in a desperate effort to avoid being charged as an accomplice to Valdez's terrorist crimes. He told "Leonard Justice" all about the arms deal arranged with Valdez. Of course, the conversation with Valdez had been taped, but Farrel added exact details about the location of the delivery that hadn't been discussed because Valdez already knew about the polluted cove.

The Farm had come through for Bolan, and it was the warrior's job to use the information. He knew when the terrorists planned to be at the pier to get their shipment of weapons and make the first payment. The warrior arrived hours in advance with Jack Grimaldi, and Ramon and Raul for backup. They had plenty of time to study the area and prepare for the enemy.

Night descended and they waited in the dark, hidden among the trees and foliage around the clearing of the pier. Bolan didn't know if the terrorists would arrive by boat, vehicle or on foot, but he hoped Valdez would be among them. The terrorist leader wouldn't escape again, the warrior vowed. This time, he was ready and fully equipped for the confrontation.

Ironically the Executioner had been supplied with everything he needed by Valdez's unsuccessful raid on the U.S. Embassy. He had helped himself to weapons left by the enemy. Bolan finally had an M-16 assault rifle with almost a thousand rounds of 5.56 mm ammunition and several spare magazines. It wasn't equipped with the M-203 grenade launcher the warrior had hoped for, but he now possessed the M-79 launcher Valdez had dropped on the pavement. He had also claimed more than a dozen M-26 fragmentation grenades and no longer had to rely on crude pipe bombs or shotgun-shell minigrenades.

Added to the Beretta 93-R and the Desert Eagle, Bolan no longer had a problem of limited firepower. Jack Grimaldi had received a Beretta 92-F among the gear sent by diplomatic pouch to the embassy, but he also carried a Heckler & Koch MP-5 submachine gun supplied from the terrorists' abandoned hardware. Ramon and Raul hadn't been trained in the use of automatic weapons. The twins were disappointed when Bolan insisted they use the weapons they were familiar with.

"I can't believe I came down here and you put me to work as a ground grunt instead of a pilot," Grimaldi groused.

He spoke in a whisper although they saw no sign of the terrorists. Bolan knew Grimaldi wasn't really complaining. He was just getting bored squatting among the ferns and bushes. It was hot and humid in the dense foliage. Insects swarmed the area, and the men were constantly assaulted by mosquitoes, deerflies and other annoying, biting pests. Occasionally something rustled among the tall grass and brush. The Executioner wasn't concerned about rats or poisonous snakes. Such creatures presented a minimal threat to human beings. The most dangerous predator to man would always be man.

"Don't need you as a pilot right now," Bolan stated. "If Valdez's crew don't show up tonight, I won't need you for anything except company."

"You think they might not show?" Grimaldi asked with a frown. "I thought Valdez and that guy in Florida closed the deal and arranged delivery time and place."

"Yeah," Bolan confirmed, "but it's possible Valdez and Farrel had previously arranged some sort of confirmation as standard procedure before carrying out a deal. Maybe one of them was supposed to call back twenty-four hours after the first call just to be sure nothing went wrong at the other end. Farrel didn't mention anything like that, but he might reckon the Feds will cut him a break if he appears to be cooperating even if we don't nail Valdez."

"Well, that's a—"

He stopped in midsentence as a pair of headlights appeared at the neglected, seldom-used dirt road. Bolan gestured for Grimaldi to move to where Ramon and Raul were located to be certain they were ready for battle.

The headlights drew closer, accompanied by the rumble of engines and the rustle of low-hanging branches being abruptly brushed aside. The shape of a large truck rolled into view, followed by a second vehicle. The rigs came to a halt by the clearing at the pier. Figures emerged from the tarp-covered back of each truck, jumping to the ground. Clad in fatigue uniforms and boots, the hardmen carried an assortment of military weapons.

The terrorists moved into position swiftly, four covering the road, others assuming guard by the tree line. Most waited by the vehicles, weapons held at port arms.

Doors to the truck cabs opened and four more figures stepped from the rigs. Bolan studied these men, hoping to see Valdez among the enemy forces. None of them appeared tall enough to be the renegade leader, but one man caught the Executioner's eye. Short, balding and soft in appearance, Hector Arguello stood out among the younger, tougher-looking members of the terrorist unit.

The 23rd September veteran was certainly one of Valdez's top lieutenants, possibly second in command of the fanatic forces. Arguello was the highest-ranking man on the pier. If they could take him alive, they might be able to force him to reveal where Valdez was and how to best take the enemy base. So far they hadn't had much luck taking any of the terrorists captive for interrogation.

The warrior found some comfort in the knowledge the enemy's streak of bad luck had been far worse. And he intended to make sure it didn't get any better.

He knelt by the trunk of a thick tree, clad in a blacksuit to blend with the shadows. The M-16 stood propped beside him, and the M-79 grenade launcher lay on the ground within easy reach. He didn't plan to use the latter. Bolan reckoned there were about two dozen terrorists on the pier, but they were less than three hundred yards away and grouped together in an area roughly the size of a basketball court. The warrior didn't want to blast the enemy to pieces. He wasn't a butcher, and he wanted live prisoners this time.

Bolan reached for a canister grenade on his belt. It was easily recognized by touch, and he had no trouble distinguishing it from the baseball-shaped M-26 fraggers. He took the canister from his belt, pulled the ring pin and tossed the grenade in a low underhand throw. The warrior shielded his face with a forearm as he headed back to his previous position.

The canister landed at the clearing and rolled to the pier. A startled voice announced the object had been spotted by the terrorists. The detonator ignited, the canister blasted apart and a magnesium core exploded in a brilliant burst of white light. The violent glare stunned and blinded the terrorists who looked at it.

Rifle shots rang out, and two of the terrorists stationed by the road suddenly convulsed from the impact of bullets. A volley of automatic fire snarled from the bush and sent two hardmen tumbling from the tree line. Bolan reached for his M-16 and quickly selected a target. Some of the enemy hadn't looked into the minimagnesium nova and still retained full ability to see and use their weapons. Bolan picked one who seemed to be trying to locate Grimaldi's position from the muzzle-flash of the pilot's MP-5.

Bolan triggered the M-16 and scored with a 3-round burst to the man's upper torso. The terrorist dropped his assault rifle and collapsed to the plank walk. Several hardmen returned fire, shooting wildly in response. Many literally fired blindly into the brush, but those able to keep their wits scrambled for cover.

HECTOR ARGUELLO DUCKED behind the cab of a truck and clutched a Mendoza submachine gun to his chest. The weapon was an unusual choice, because none of the other terrorists carried a Mendoza and Arguello only had two spare magazines for the Mexican-manufactured chopper. The Mendoza was used almost exclusively by the *federales* and had never gained much popularity with the national police, who tended to favor firearms made in the United States or European models.

Although he knew the Mendoza wasn't a very practical weapon, Arguello had kept the gun for more than fifteen years. He had taken it from a dead *federal*, killed in a gun battle with the 23rd September members in his cell. Arguello had secretly considered the Mendoza to be a sort of good-luck piece. He decided this superstition was pretty stupid as he crouched by the vehicle.

A voice bellowed from a bullhorn somewhere among the trees and bushes. It ordered them in Spanish to surrender. They were warned to put down their guns, raise their hands and step into the open. The voice added that the pier was surrounded, and they would be slaughtered if they tried to resist.

One of the younger, hotheaded members of the terrorist band responded by swinging his assault rifle around the end of the truck he used for shelter and blasting a short salvo at the trees. His head suddenly recoiled and he dropped to the planks, his skull shattered by at least two high-velocity projectiles.

"We have to get out of here," a man near Arguello declared. "I'll drive this truck—"

"We'll never make it that way," Arguello said, cutting him off. "They'll hit the trucks with grenades the moment one moves."

"Maybe they don't have grenades."

"They already used a flash grenade of some kind and they're armed with automatic weapons," the veteran terrorist stated. "Better assume they've got hand grenades. They were obviously expecting us. Bastards may even have Claymore mines rigged or some other type explosives set at this pier."

"What do we do?"

"I'll try to distract them," Arguello replied. "They haven't fired many shots and I haven't been able to get an accurate estimate as to how many may be in their group, but I don't think there are more than six or seven of them. We may even be dealing with that damn American that Valdez has been fretting about."

"I hope he's out there," the younger man said with a cruel smile. "It will be a pleasure to stand over that Anglo pig and piss on his dead body."

"We have to kill him first," Arguello reminded the anxious youth. "Get eight or nine men together. Make certain their vision has cleared well enough to see where the hell they're going. Then spread them out, tell them to stay low and be prepared to crawl on their bellies to the forest."

Arguello gave the man a few minutes to contact the others while he opened the passenger-side door to a truck cab and reached inside. The terrorist took a large aluminum case from the front seat, tossed it onto the hood of the truck and hastily tied a white handkerchief to the barrel of his Mendoza.

"*¡Bandera blanca!*" Arguello called out. "White flag! Hold your fire! Let's talk! *¿Comprende?*"

No reply came from the forest. Arguello rose slowly and held the improvised banner high, one hand gripping the buttstock of the Mendoza chopper and the other hand empty and open.

"I don't know who you are or why you are doing this," he began in Spanish, "but there is five hundred thousand dollars in American money in this case. Five hundred thousand dollars. That's a lot of money. How much do you get paid at the end of the week or the end of the month? How much will each of you get if you split five hundred thousand dollars equally among yourselves? Seventy thousand dollars? Perhaps eighty or even one hundred thousand each?"

He glanced at the ground and saw several figures in a prone position, weapons cradled in the crooks of their elbows as they started to slowly crawl toward the tree line.

"All you have to do to get this money is let us go," Arguello continued. "Just let us climb into the trucks and drive away. We'll leave the money for you. Tell whoever you work for we managed to escape. Such an easy way to make so much money...."

There was still no reply. Arguello started to repeat the proposition in English, to make certain the others understood and to try to buy more time for the terrorist troops to reach the trees. He became more confident of his safety and moved to the nose of the cab to open the case so the invisible enemy could see the stacks of money inside.

"You'd better answer me!" Arguello warned. "If you don't agree to my terms, I'll burn the money! So if you think you can kill us and take it..."

Gunfire erupted from the brush. Bullets ripped into the bodies of the terrorists crawling toward the tree line. Corpses rolled from the impact of the slugs. Other members of the terrorist group returned fire, trying to locate Bolan and his team by the muzzle-flashes of their weapons. Three metal eggs hurtled from the foliage, hitting the pier and rolling to the trucks."

"Damn it all!" Arguello exclaimed.

The grenades exploded with a violent shock wave that sent one truck tumbling onto its side. Voices screamed as shrapnel tore flesh. Bodies were thrown across the pier, bloodied and mutilated by the blasts. Arguello was pitched to the plank walk, rolling forcibly until he crashed into the base of the toolshed. His vision blurred and a dark veil seemed to hover over him. The terrorist's right shoulder ached, and he was aware he lost the grip on his Mendoza.

Arguello shook his head to try to fight off the dark mist of unconsciousness that seemed about to claim him. The pain in his shoulder suddenly increased, and more pain lanced his side as he tried to rise. His right hand and arm wouldn't obey commands from his brain. Arguello fearfully glanced at his limb, afraid it might have been torn off by the explosion.

He was relieved to see the arm remained attached, although twisted in an unnatural manner. His shoulder had been dislocated by the fall. The terrorist blinked his eyes to clear his vision and saw the Mendoza subgun four or five yards away. So much for the "lucky" firearm, Arguello thought bitterly.

He glanced about. A number of his comrades seemed to be dead or seriously wounded. Two or more were pinned under the overturned truck. One terrified man rushed to the end of the pier and dived into the water, unmindful of the thick oil slick. The idiot would be lucky if he didn't drown in the black crude.

Arguello slumped into a seated position, his back against the toolshed wall. Few of his comrades remained. Two ran for the abandoned, rotted shop. This appeared to be the best available cover, but it seemed obvious to Arguello it wouldn't be good enough. If the enemy could blast the trucks with grenades, they could surely destroy the crumbling old wooden structure as well. Some die-hard fanatics stayed by the trucks, yet most of these appeared to still be half-blind from the magnesium burst. They hadn't moved because they simply didn't know what else to do.

Two members of the group sent to the trees had avoided the hail of gunfire that cut down most of their comrades. They continued to move into the brush, following Arguello's strategy. Bushes stirred and a head and shoulders rose by the trunk of a tree. The terrorist pair quickly swung their weapons at the figure and opened fire. Bullets hammered the unlucky target into the tree and split his shirtfront with a jagged pattern of bloodied holes.

Too late they recognized the fatigue clothing and the now-lifeless face of one of their own comrades. The gunmen had made more than one mistake when they fired on the dazed figure. They had also betrayed their position to the Executioner.

A salvo of M-16 rounds hit one terrorist in the chest and pitched his body backward into the clearing. The man performed an awkward back roll and sprawled on his belly. His corpse twitched slightly and lay still. The second gunman dropped to a kneeling stance and tried to fire at Bolan's position. Another 3-round burst of 5.56 mm projectiles drilled into his face and forehead before he could trigger a single shot.

"Last chance to give it up!" a voice shouted in English. "We don't want to kill the rest of you, but we can and will if you don't surrender now!"

Arguello watched as his comrades made their choice to surrender or die. One by one, they threw down their weapons and raised their hands. They stepped into clear view and urged the enemy not to fire. Some spoke this plea in English as well as Spanish.

"I suppose it had to end this way eventually," Arguello muttered to himself as he leaned forward.

His left hand pulled up a pant leg. The cuff rose above the rosewood grips of a small over-under derringer jammed in his boot. Arguello drew the diminutive pistol. It held only two shots, but each cartridge was a .41 Magnum. He had carried the little hideout gun for years without ever using it except for target practice. It didn't have much range due to the short barrel.

That hardly mattered under the circumstances. Arguello considered waiting for the enemy to show themselves. If he played dead, he might be able to lure one of them to come close enough to take him out with the derringer. Not likely, he decided. Whoever they were, the unseen opponents didn't make many mistakes. Maybe they were Farrel's people. The damn gunrunner could have decided to double-cross his former partner. They could have set up the ambush so they could keep the guns and take the money....

No, Arguello thought. The arms dealers wouldn't be interested in taking prisoners, and they probably would have responded to Arguello's offer to take the money. Yet at least one of them spoke English with an accent that was certainly American. It was the one Valdez had spoken of, the tall commando.

"Doesn't really matter now," he decided as he raised the derringer.

Arguello opened his mouth and stuck the gun between his teeth. The hard steel muzzle touched the roof of his mouth. Hector Arguello didn't hesitate. He squeezed the trigger.

11

"Do you guys always make such a mess?" Karl Brunjes asked.

The CIA man addressed Mack Bolan and Jack Grimaldi in a small soundproof conference room at the United States embassy. Ellena Santos sat at the long wooden table. Colonel Roberto Gonzalez was also present. Although he was dressed in a dark gray suit, white shirt and tie, his appearance would have labeled him as a military man even if he hadn't been introduced with a field-grade rank. Gonzalez's hair was clipped short, his mustache trimmed to a narrow line that didn't stray beyond the upper lip. He sat ramrod straight, his posture developed by years of military drill and ceremony.

"At least this time you managed to take some of the terrorists alive," Gonzalez remarked. "I hope I do not sound too critical, Mr. Belasko. After all, you have had far more success than we dealing with Valdez and his followers."

Gonzalez didn't say who "we" referred to. Both Brunjes and Ellena knew him, so the colonel was obviously involved with Mexico internal security and law enforcement.

"A few things worked in our favor this time," Bolan began. "We knew exactly where and when the terrorists would show and the location was far from any innocent bystanders. They weren't expecting a trap. None of them was armed with grenade or rocket launchers or even hand grenades. They didn't bring a lot of firepower because they thought they'd be buying an arsenal."

"They didn't get the guns or the money," Brunjes added. "The five hundred thousand dollars intended for the arms deal has been returned, Colonel. Most of it anyway. Some of the cash was scattered across the pier when the trucks were hit by explosions."

"That was reported to me, Karl," Gonzalez stated. "Thank you. The money is not a major concern to us. Unfortunately Valdez still has one and a half million dollars to finance his private army. Correct?"

"Something like that," Ellena replied. "Part of what was stolen in Acapulco was jewelry worth hundreds of thousands of dollars. Valdez will probably try to fence the gems for cash. It's unlikely he'll get more than a quarter what their value is supposed to be."

"Even if you figure Valdez has more or less a million bucks on hand," Grimaldi remarked, "that's still a nice nest egg, and he can always steal more."

"Valdez still has enough money to stay in business," Bolan said. "He went to Farrel first because he was an easy source and he thought he could put together a large arms deal in a hurry. There are other gunrunners. Valdez might do business with some South American outfit next time. It won't be so easy to cut off his source and ambush his people again. He was too eager and he got careless. Don't expect him to do that again."

"His forces must be growing smaller," Gonzalez stated. "How many men can he have left at this point?"

"Some of his followers are women," the Executioner said. "We don't know what the total of his remaining force is, but an educated guess would be no less than thirty and probably no more than sixty. Most likely somewhere in the middle. Say about forty-five. If we're lucky, some people will decide to abandon ship and leave his outfit after Arguello doesn't come home with the weapons they wanted. If we're not so lucky, he may have been able to recruit more followers."

"He may even hire mercenaries from Guatemala," Brunjes added. "Valdez is probably located near the border, and everybody knows how bad things are in Guatemala. Average income down there is less than nine hundred dollars a year. You could probably find a lot of killers-for-rent for about two grand each who are willing to 'join the revolution' for a couple months."

"That's a rather disturbing thought," Gonzalez admitted. "Speaking of where Valdez is located, do you finally have an idea where that might be?"

"So far, the terrorists captured at the pier haven't been very cooperative from what I've learned," Ellena said. "A number of them are hospitalized with injuries. The men held in maximum security don't seem willing to betray Valdez.''

"Too bad you couldn't bring in Arguello,'' Brunjes said. ''I would have guessed that sly old fox would have been smart enough to try to make a deal for a reduced sentence by offering to turn state's witness against Valdez. Guess his loyalty to the revolution— even if it wasn't the Marxist one he joined when he was a youth—proved greater for him in the end.''

"Back to your question,'' Bolan said to the colonel. "We do have a good idea where Valdez's secret base is located. Thanks to satellite surveillance from our connections in the U.S., groups of individuals were tracked by heat-sensor devices and enhanced radio-telemetry moving through tropical rain forest regions in the Yucatán. This is farther east than where Valdez was originally believed to be based.''

"The Yucatán?'' Gonzalez asked with a frown. "Are you sure of this? How reliable are these sources?''

"Extremely reliable,'' Bolan assured him. "I can't explain how our organization works or any details about it. That's top secret on the highest level. I can tell you the information comes from monitoring NSA SIGINT spy satellites, which you probably know are the most advanced in the world. We also get information from CIA, ONI, Air Force Intelligence and other surveillance satellites.''

"Hell, Colonel,'' Grimaldi added, "we even get data from spy satellites of other countries. Trust us, our sources are about as close to perfect as you're going to find in an imperfect world.''

"I think we can trust your word based on what you've done so far," Brunjes said. "Well, it may be a little late in the game to get the full cooperation from everyone that you deserved from the start of your mission, but you've got it now, Belasko."

"That's why I'm here," Gonzalez confirmed. "My government is prepared to give you any and all assistance necessary. I can assign a battalion of troops to carry out a raid on the enemy base. Tell us where they are, and we'll be glad to take care of them."

"Your offer has an appeal," Bolan replied, "but I don't think that's the way to get Valdez. He's avoided the police, military and *federales,* over and over again. Valdez is an expert in jungle combat and his followers are mostly Indians, born and raised in the tropical rain forest. You send in a fleet of helicopters, the terrorists will hear them before the choppers come within ten kilometers of the base. Attempts to find cocaine labs operating in the jungle in Colombia and Bolivia have repeatedly failed when helicopters were used."

"But you were sent because you're an expert helicopter pilot," the colonel said to Grimaldi.

"And I know the disadvantages and limitations of a helicopter as well. You can move in and out, up and down in a chopper better than anything else. But it isn't silent and it's not invisible. I can serve as an air taxi to save our guys some boot leather, and I can provide air support if needed and pick them up after the battle. That's why I'm here."

"How many troops can you carry in a single helicopter?" Gonzalez asked. "You can't plan to attack an enemy base holding thirty or more armed terrorists without adequate forces."

"A large number of troops tramping through the rain forest would be almost as obvious as a squadron of choppers," Bolan replied. "The only way to do this and be sure we get Valdez is to go in with the minimum force necessary to do the job. It's not machismo, Colonel. Sometimes smaller is better."

"Sounds like you're flirting with suicide as well," Gonzalez said with a frown. "You intend to go after them by yourself? That's insane."

"Not exactly," Bolan replied. "Ramon and Raul will go with me. They know the Yucatán and they know Indians who live there. That's another reason not to use your troops. Sorry, Colonel, but the military isn't very popular with the people who live in the rain forest. The government has been assisting big business that's been chopping down the trees and seizing land the Indians consider their home. They're not going to be very cooperative with your soldiers."

"My government has been doing its best to help those people improve their standard of living," Gonzalez insisted. "In order to do that we need that cooperation between government and big business, including cooperation with businesses and trade in your country. That way our economy is better and we can provide more jobs and services. The Indians will benefit as well. Members of the regular Zapatistas want improved medical treatment, education and better jobs. Yet they think we should do this without expanding industry and lumber operations in the rain forests."

"This isn't a political debate," the Executioner said. "We're not here to change or argue about government policies or Mexico's internal problems. I'm just explaining why your soldiers are regarded as the enemy by many of the Indians living in the rain forest. They may not like what Valdez is doing, but he isn't trying to claim their homeland, cut down thousands of trees for timber and all the other actions by your government and major corporations that they consider oppressive."

"Maybe we could go into the jungle disguised as a group of researchers with *National Geographic* or something like that," Brunjes suggested. "Have to hide all those guns and stuff. Make the gear look like camera equipment and supplies."

"You're volunteering for this mission?" Gonzalez asked with surprise.

"I know I'm an Anglo and can't pass for anything else," the CIA man replied, "but two white Americans won't seem suspicious with the right cover. My Spanish is a lot better than Belasko's, and I've been to the Yucatán to see the remains of the Mayan civilization."

"We appreciate the offer, Karl," Bolan said, "but you're not going. You're brave enough. You proved that during the attack on the embassy. That doesn't change the fact you've got old injuries that keep you from being physically prepared for combat. Ramon and Raul lack the degree of training and experience I'd prefer for a mission like this, but they know the region very well—not just from a tour to the Mayan ruins. Of course, they speak Spanish and they have working vocabularies of some of the local Indian languages as well. That makes them better qualified for this task than a company of paratroopers who've never set foot in the Yucatán.''

"And they don't have any physical problems," Brunjes added, clearly disappointed with the rejection. "Okay. I guess I'll do what I can from the sidelines."

"What can we do if we don't supply troops or air support?" Gonzalez asked. "I'm beginning to think there's no reason for me to even be here."

"I need the work done on preparing that gunship," Grimaldi stated. "And I need it finished damn soon. We gotta move before those sons of bitches decide to strike camp and head for a new location."

"That doesn't give us much time," Bolan added. "Arguello was probably supposed to report back to Valdez by radio to let him know how the arms deal turned out. Valdez must already suspect Arguello and the others won't be coming back. He won't wait long because he knows eventually any prisoner will talk if subjected to the right kind of pressure. He'll assume this time we managed to take a few of his people alive."

"Valdez must use radio contact for people in the field," Ellena remarked. "I would assume he certainly has radio frequencies monitored. Especially military and police broadcasts if he can get them.''

"Hell," Brunjes said. "Truck drivers pick up police radio wavelengths on their CBs, so I'm sure Valdez has equipment at least that sophisticated.''

"He does," Bolan confirmed. "His men used handheld motion- or heat-detector units to search the area at the Elizondo auto shop. If he has gear like that, he definitely has a radio-monitor system setup as well.''

"But Arguello and the others did not use any detection devices at the pier," Gonzalez remarked. "Perhaps Valdez is not as well supplied with exotic electrical devices as you think.''

"He probably doesn't have a lot of high-tech equipment to spare, and he didn't think Arguello would have any real problems getting the weapons shipment," Grimaldi explained. "After all, Farrel was Valdez's partner in crime and they'd never had any trouble smuggling in arms that way before. Why use the detectors if they might be needed at home base?''

"It is best we assume Valdez does listen to radio broadcasts for information and to gather intelligence for his plans," Ellena declared. "So perhaps we can feed him some story that will make him believe he is safer than he really is.''

"Misinformation as we call it in the trade," Brunjes said with a nod of approval. "We can have the military broadcast a report that all of the terrorists were killed at the pier. No survivors. Might even tell that story to the press so it'll be on the regular radio news broadcasts. Give it to UPI. Wouldn't be the first fake story to be heard around the world.''

"Spoken like a real Company man," Grimaldi said dryly.

"Giving a story like that to the general media might make Valdez more suspicious," Bolan said. "The incident at the pier occurred far from the eye of the public. Since the press would only know what the military and the government wanted them to know, it's unlikely they'd be told simply that a group of two dozen terrorists were killed and none taken prisoner. Usually such offerings to the media by 'insiders' are phrased as 'soldiers defeated rebel forces in armed conflict. Undetermined number of terrorists dead and no casualties reported by the other side.' Details aren't generally given until the source decides exactly how much it wants to share.''

"This time the people in this room are the 'source,''' Gonzalez stated. "What do you suggest we share?''

"Don't go to the media," the Executioner replied. "Use military or police wavelengths and use a frequency that seems surreptitious. As if they don't want the media to know about it yet. Claim the terrorists were stopped by a patrol on the road near the pier. Say the enemy trucks were destroyed by grenades during a firefight, most of the terrorists were killed except for a couple that are comatose and not expected to live and an undetermined number that managed to escape into the rain forest. Give a very general description of the fugitives. Dressed in fatigue-style clothing, probably young males because they moved rapidly and they're armed with automatic weapons. Add that one was seen carrying some sort of metal case. No idea what it might contain, but believed it could be some sort of explosives, sniper rifle or radio-communications unit."

"So you want Valdez to believe his people were probably hit before they could buy the guns," Brunjes said, "but they might have gotten away with that aluminum case filled with money. That would give him a reason to stay put for a while. A chance that five hundred thousand dollars might come back to his bankroll seems like a good reason to me."

"Yeah," Grimaldi said. "Hard to say how long he'll wait. He might be suspicious of the story or he might figure whoever grabbed the cash might have decided to keep it for himself. Still, he ought to stay put for at least a day or two. That should be enough."

"It better be," Bolan stated. "We won't have more than two days to find Valdez's base and shut him down for good."

"How exactly do you plan to do that, Mr. Belasko?" Gonzalez asked. "Do you intend to kill them all?"

"If we can take prisoners, Grissim will radio your troops and they can come in with choppers to pick up captives. But I doubt that will happen. We might not have to kill all of them. If a few of them choose to run, we'll probably let them go. Just as long as we get Valdez and destroy his operation our mission will be complete. I don't object to taking Valdez alive, but that's unlikely. He must know how this will eventually end. Valdez is so full of anger and bitterness it's become his whole life. He lives only for revenge against the U.S. government for what he regards as abuse of Hispanics. His survival instincts and training saved his life twice, but he really intends to die for his cause. Valdez may not realize it, but he actually wants to be a martyr.''

''An interesting psychological evaluation,'' Ellena commented. ''After what happened to my brother, I hope Valdez gets his wish and spends the rest of eternity in hell.''

''What happens to his soul is up to whatever happens after death,'' the Executioner replied. ''But I'm going to see to his final judgment in this life.''

12

Adolfo Valdez cleaned and oiled his disassembled Heckler & Koch submachine gun. He wanted the weapon in perfect working condition. Everything was going badly and promised to get even worse. He had to be prepared for trouble.

Perez, the communications officer, reported hearing a message on a special shortwave military frequency that claimed two trucks had encountered a patrol of soldiers. A firefight occurred, the trucks were destroyed and most of the men with the vehicles had been killed. The claim that a few escaped, including one carrying a metal case, suggested a handful of the group sent to make the arms purchase might be headed back to base with the money intended for the deal.

Valdez doubted this. The story seemed too precise. Mention of the aluminum case made him suspicious. It wasn't likely that it would have been noticed in a fierce battle in a jungle at night.

The story was probably false, but there was a slim chance it was true. Valdez realized Perez had received the information from one of his radio-monitor personnel. This meant the rest of the camp knew about it as well. Valdez suspected some of his own troops were ready to mutiny. They had seen too many of their comrades killed recently, and too many of Valdez's plans had failed. Many, perhaps most, had lost faith in his leadership. Some of them would have already turned on Valdez if they didn't fear his personal skill as a warrior or hope to get part of the war chest.

The frightened followers would try to leave the base and flee into the jungle, Valdez thought. The greedy members wouldn't confront him until they were certain the case with $500,000 wasn't coming back. Then they would demand the remaining one and a half million dollars in cash and jewelry be given to them...or they'd simply kill him and take it for themselves. Some would remain loyal to Valdez, but he doubted enough would stand by him to defeat an attack by the majority.

He glanced around the canvas walls of his tent as he sat by the field desk, hastily reassembling the H&K subgun. As if he didn't have enough problems to deal with from the *federales,* the military and whatever the combined governments of Mexico and the United States pitted against him, he now had to worry about his own people. Valdez hadn't felt so vulnerable since his release from prison.

The terrorist leader finished putting the MP-5 together and reached for a magazine loaded with 9 mm Parabellum rounds. He shoved it into the well and chambered a round. Valdez felt better with the weapon ready, yet he realized any sense of safety to be an illusion. If those around him wanted him dead, they could kill him by simply surrounding the tent and blasting it with automatic weapons. At least his old prison cell had concrete walls. Canvas wouldn't stop a bullet.

Valdez ran the long blade of his machete across a sharpening steel. He wanted every weapon ready for action. They had seen him kill García in the duel and appreciated his ability with the big jungle knife. Satisfied with the sharp edge, he wiped the metal with a light coat of oil and slid the machete into a belt scabbard. He would carry it with him at all times. The big knife would be no match for a gun at ten paces, but at least it would serve as a reminder to his troops that Valdez was a true fighting man.

He had never cared much for pistols and didn't have much faith in his ability with a handgun. Valdez had never done well on a pistol range and favored a submachine gun or shotgun for close-quarters combat. Yet he was considering carrying a sidearm in the future.

That damn gringo commando was certainly an expert marksman with a pistol, Valdez thought bitterly. He recalled the confrontation with the mysterious warrior during the battle at the U.S. embassy. The bastard used a shotgun just as skillfully as he had handled that big, powerful handgun that brought down more than one of Valdez's troops. Whoever he was, the Anglo seemed to have exceptional talent with instruments of war and death. He had used a rifle and grenades with lethal efficiency at the auto-repair shop.

Valdez prided himself on his combat skills, but this stranger was certainly his equal. In some ways he was a better warrior than Valdez. Probably a better strategist as well. Of course, someone else might have planned strategy for the commando and he was simply sent to carry out orders like some sort of deadly android programmed for war. Yet Valdez sensed the man was more than that. Everything had gone well until that night at the shop. He felt as if his intelligence, skill and machismo had been put to the test by the warrior and he had failed again and again.

Valdez had gotten himself into this situation. It had been his choice to come to Mexico and carry out a murderous campaign against U.S. citizens—most of whom had nothing to do with the government he despised, and none of whom was involved in making decisions on foreign policy. The fact he had killed more Mexican nationals than Americans didn't disturb him. Or that his followers who had believed in him and obeyed him with fanatical loyalty had been slaughtered due to his commands.

Valdez didn't blame himself or regard his behavior as being the cause of so much death and misery, or the reason he now felt threatened even by his own terrorist minions. Instead, he felt the mystery commando was the single person most responsible for his decline and eventual downfall. Valdez had no illusions that he would succeed. He knew the end was near and he wouldn't survive.

That left only one last goal. Valdez wanted revenge. This desire had motivated him to come to

Mexico for his demented campaign of violence and it continued to do so. The focus had changed from striking out at the United States to eliminating an individual. He hoped he would have one more confrontation with the Anglo warrior. If he had to lose his own life, he wanted to take that gringo bastard with him to the grave.

JACK GRIMALDI'S GUNSHIP was ready. The Bell helicopter had been equipped with twin machine guns at the nose and braces of multimissile launchers under the hull. Heat sensors, light-intensity amplification night-vision gear, an advanced radar system were all linked to a computer installed at the control panel. Armor plating and reinforced Plexiglas would stand up to repeated salvos of intense heavy gunfire, but the gunship wasn't invincible. A well-placed round from a rocket launcher could blast it out of the sky.

The Stony Man pilot sat at the controls as the big rotor blade whirled in preparation for flight. Ramon and Raul entered the open sliding door to the Bell copter. They wore green-and-brown camouflage fatigues, combat boots and caps. Each twin carried a short-barreled Winchester pump shotgun with extra shells, and a .38 Smith & Wesson revolver was holstered at each man's hip. Large machete jungle knives hung from belt sheaths. Raul, the better rifleman of the pair, also had a Marlin rifle with a shoulder strap. Both carried backpacks, canteens and hand grenades.

Mack Bolan prepared to enter the chopper. Clad in jungle fatigues and wearing a floppy brim "boonie" hat, the warrior was rigged for war. The formidable Beretta 93-R was in shoulder leather and the powerful .44 Magnum Desert Eagle was holstered on his right hip. A U.S. Army machete hung by his left hip, and his Ka-bar combat knife was strapped to his right calf just above the paratrooper boot. He carried the M-16 by the "handle" above the receiver, and the M-79 grenade launcher was sheathed in a specially made leather scabbard attached to his backpack. His belt was loaded with magazine pouches for the weapons, and he had a supply of 40 mm shells for the M-79, as well as hand grenades.

"My God," Karl Brunjes had remarked. "You're really gonna carry all that on a trek through the jungle that could take nearly two days?"

"If it can keep you alive, it's not too heavy," the warrior replied.

The CIA man stood at the helipad as Bolan boarded the gunship. Colonel Gonzalez and Ellena Santos had also come to see the four-man fighting unit depart. Conversation was sparse. There was little left to be said as the final phase of the mission went into action. The time for planning, arguing and speculation was over. Success or failure depended on the courage and skill of the Executioner and his three allies.

Gonzalez brought his heels together and raised his hand to the bill of his cap in a solemn salute. Bolan knew this wasn't an insincere gesture. The field-grade officer expressed genuine respect and honored the soldier from the United States whom he knew only by the cover name Belasko. Bolan assumed the attention position and returned the salute with the dignity it deserved.

"Okay," he called to Grimaldi as he stepped aboard the helicopter and shut the door. "Let's do it."

13

The Yucatán Peninsula is one of the greatest tropical regions of Central America. On the map it resembles the head of a large seal mounted on the borders of Guatemala and Belize. The Gulf of Mexico meets the northwestern shores and the Caribbean Sea the southeast. The Yucatán Channel flows between the tip of the peninsula and the island of Cuba.

The waters along the shoreline have always been important. They had been a major trade route for the Mayans during their Classic period from A.D. 300 to 900. Shipping continued along these pathways for lumber companies, mining operations and import-export interests for the United States, Central and South America.

As the helicopter slowly descended and cruised above a column of banana trees, Mack Bolan recalled these details about the geographical features and history of the Yucatán, which Brunjes had told him. If the guy decided to leave the CIA he had the potential to get a new career as a geography teacher, the warrior thought. Yet Bolan had appreciated Brunjes's little lectures about Mexico. Any information about a country and its people could be useful during a mission.

He gazed down at the clusters of large banana leaves and spotted a clearing below. Bolan judged the distance to the ground to be about thirty yards and the area for the landing roughly nine or ten yards in diameter. He turned to Ramon and Raul. Neither man seemed comfortable flying in the chopper, but they clearly didn't like the idea of leaving the craft while it remained in the sky.

Bolan had instructed them in the procedure for rappelling from the copter, but there hadn't been enough time to practice under proper training conditions.

The trio wore harnesses for the task with carabiners attached, ropes running through the metal rings. Bolan pushed a coil of rope from the chopper. The line descended to the ground below, the other end fixed to the hull of the craft.

"Okay," Valdez announced. "You're first."

"No me gusto..." Ramon began before switching to English. "I do not like this."

"It's not as hard as it seems or as dangerous," Bolan assured him. "Just hold the line the way I showed you, step back to the exit and plant your feet at the edge."

Ramon reluctantly obeyed. He clung to the rope tightly and hesitantly eased a foot back to grope for the rim. Bolan grabbed his arm to reassure him and gently pushed him back. Ramon swallowed hard and moved his other foot into position. He stood at the threshold, body whipped by the air current of the rotor blade, fists locked to the rope and legs straight, boot soles braced on the edge.

"Now bend your knees and kick off."

Ramon froze in place. His head lowered to stare between his legs at the rope and the ground far below.

"Don't look down," Bolan said. "We don't have all day, Ramon. Kick off, work the rope and let the harness do the rest. Your feet will touch ground before you know it."

"Yes," Ramon replied grimly. "Maybe too fast." But he pushed with his feet and swung clear of the craft. He dropped from view, only his hands on the taut rope still visible. Ramon hung on, legs flailing until he found the skid to the helicopter landing gear. He stood on it, reluctant to push off and continue the descent. Bolan figured he would have to climb onto the skid himself to get Ramon off it, but the man finally pushed off and rappelled slowly down the line.

"Raul," Bolan told the other twin, "your turn."

"My brother had better be unharmed," Raul replied with a hard edge to his voice.

"Get down there and check on him," the Executioner said.

Raul also hesitated, but he was quicker out of the chopper than his brother had been. Bolan watched him rappel to the skid and descend his rope in a gradual, jerky climb to the ground.

"You'll have this bird to yourself now, Jack," Bolan called to Grimaldi.

The pilot turned his head to look at the warrior, hands still busy with the controls, feet working the rudders. Maintaining a hover with a helicopter required a fair amount of constant effort with virtually all four limbs involved, but Grimaldi had done this so often the task was no more complex for him than walking from a mailbox and opening a letter at the same time.

"Take care, Sarge," Grimaldi replied. "It's a jungle down there."

"Everywhere is a jungle these days," Bolan said.

"Stay in touch," Grimaldi urged. "Give a call if you need any help."

"Don't worry about that," the warrior answered.

Bolan jumped, feeling the tug of the rotor blade current as he leapt clear of the craft. He plunged past the landing skids before he grabbed the rappelling rope. He held it with one hand and scooped up the line running between his legs with the other. Bolan allowed the carabiners to slide along the rope and easily descended to the ground. The chore was so familiar to the warrior it offered no more challenge than sliding down a pole to a veteran fireman.

Ramon and Raul seemed stunned by Bolan's expertise. Their hands were still too unsteady to unbuckle their harnesses after the jump. The Executioner had removed his gear before the twins could do the same.

"First time is the hardest," Bolan assured them. "Do it often enough and there's nothing to it."

"Once was enough for me," Ramon replied.

The ropes ascended to the helicopter, drawn by an automated spool powered by Grimaldi's control panel. The Bell chopper rose higher, turned in the sky and soon disappeared from their view.

"We're really on our own now," Ramon said, still staring at the sky as if he expected the craft to circle back for them.

"Pretty much," Bolan replied. "We have radio contact with Grissim and we can get support, but it won't come in a blink of an eye. Don't count on anybody to get us out of a tight spot except each other."

He examined their surroundings. Bolan was no stranger to tropical rain forests. Previous missions had sent him to jungles around the world. He didn't find the environment itself frightening. Natural beauty stood everywhere. Majestic trees bore flowers and fruit. Birds sang a variety of musical warbles, chirps and whistles. Tall grass and ferns might conceal snakes or hunting big cats, but the risk from such creatures was minimal. Malaria or yellow fever from mosquitoes presented a greater threat than any nonhuman predators in the jungle.

Bolan removed a compass and three maps from a side pouch of his backpack. The maps had been produced by computer graphics, based on data collected by the Stony Man Farm team from the high-tech spy satellites. Aaron Kurtzman had faxed the special maps to Bolan. The charts concerned only the area of the Yucatán they needed to travel to reach the probable location of Valdez's secret base, supplemented by data from the Stony Man supercomputer system concerning precise details and landmarks to guide them on their search.

"Okay, gentlemen," Bolan announced. "We have to head southeast, toward the center of the peninsula. It'll be close to one hundred kilometers, but better figure most of the terrain will be difficult. We'll want to cover as much area as possible before dark."

"Ramon and I have spent a great deal of time in the Yucatán," Raul declared. "It is easy to get lost here."

"We'll come across the first landmark after we cover fifteen kilometers," Bolan explained. "Not likely we'll miss it if we're headed in the right direction."

THEY HAD NO TROUBLE finding the landmark Bolan spoke of. It was the great Mayan pyramid at Etzná. A magnificent archaeological site, the huge stone structure had endured centuries of weather and molestation by looters in search of gold relics. The building consisted of six sections with a flight of steps built across the center from top to bottom.

Ramon and Raul were familiar with such Mayan ruins, yet they were still impressed by the pyramid. Bolan found the massive, beautifully constructed site a bizarre vision surrounded by the dense foliage of the jungle. Moss and vines clung to the stone walls, grass sprouted from cracks in the ancient stairs.

The Executioner and the twins couldn't venture close enough to the pyramid to examine it in detail. Archaeological teams, tourists and various small merchants occupied the Etzná site. Three armed men would certainly attract attention. *Federales* had been sent there to protect visitors due to recent terrorist activity. It would be deadly irony to be shot at by the Mexican troops because they were mistaken for enemy terrorists prowling the jungle.

The trio continued to move toward the center of the peninsula. As Bolan expected, the jungle became more difficult to travel the farther they moved from the coastal regions, well-known Mayan sites and the major villages. They drew machetes and hacked through tangled vines and dense brush. The foliage became so thick, the tree branches so plentiful, sunlight was partially blocked from their view.

"How will we know if we reach the next landmark?" Ramon inquired as he swung his jungle knife. "We can't see anything past this crap."

"The crap *is* the landmark," Bolan answered. "Going through it instead of around will save us time, and we'll avoid some of the villages in the area that may be populated by Valdez's henchmen or sympathizers."

"And we wondered how well you would handle the Yucatán," Ramon remarked. "You managed to find one of the worst damn parts of the rain forest. I don't recall coming across anything quite this bad before."

Raul grunted as he chopped down a large fern, woven into a mat of low branches and tall grass by vine tendrils.

"We've come across tougher areas," he told his brother, "but we always had the good sense to avoid them instead of trying to cut through them."

"We should be halfway through this mess," Bolan assured them. "We ought to be in a more favorable environment after another half hour or so."

An hour later they were still slashing their way through the clogged collage of dense vegetation. The twins didn't complain, unwilling to admit they were approaching exhaustion from the difficult chore. Their companion amazed them. He chopped through heavy foliage as if he had handled a machete since childhood.

A loud growl suddenly erupted from somewhere within the wall of tangled plant life. Bolan swiftly drew the .44 Magnum and dropped to one knee, pistol in one hand and machete in the other. The twins grabbed their shotguns and glanced about, prepared for attack by the unseen beast.

"Jaguar?" Bolan asked, voice barely a whisper.

"Yes," Ramon answered. "And it's close. No more than two or three meters from the sound it made."

"It may have moved closer since it made that sound."

Bolan knew jaguars to be the largest and most powerful big cats in the Western Hemisphere. Like most wild animals, jaguars tended to avoid humans, but any creature decked with killing claws, carnivore teeth and plenty of muscle was potentially dangerous.

"I don't hear it now," Bolan said. "Maybe it's gone."

"Maybe not," Raul replied.

"Why would a jaguar be digging around in dense brush like this?" Bolan asked. "After a rabbit or something?"

"We're here," Ramon replied. "I just hope it isn't a she-cat trying to find her cubs. Never come between a mother jaguar and her young."

"I always try to avoid that," the Executioner said dryly. "We can't stand here all night waiting for the cat to show itself when it might not even be there. I'll start cutting again. You guys watch for the jaguar."

Bolan holstered his Desert Eagle and swung the machete. Sharp steel sliced through a netlike bundle of vines and bushes that had grown into one another. No growls responded to the sound of the jungle knife. Encouraged, Bolan continued to chop at the brush. He was surprised to discover the task required only a few more swings.

They emerged into a quiet area with soft mud sucking at their boot soles. A stream flowed from the north, apparently an extension of a river in the distance. Bolan recalled this feature from the maps and knew they were still headed in the right direction.

"*¡Mira!*" Raul declared as he pointed at an object by the muddy bank.

The others looked and saw the large, bulky corpse of an animal that resembled a giant pig. Bolan stepped closer and noticed the dead beast had a neck and legs longer than those of a hog. The head and ears were vaguely similar to those of a small horse, but the snout looked like the stump of an elephant trunk.

"A tapir." Ramon identified the slain animal. "Rare to find them in the Yucatán. Tapirs are usually found in South America. They live by rivers and spend much of their time in water."

The animal's head lay at an odd angle across a thick shoulder. Bolan guessed its neck had been broken. Blood still trickled from a deep gash in the tapir's belly. Claw marks formed gouges in lifeless flesh. Bolan glanced down at paw prints in the mud.

"We know what that jaguar was doing," he remarked. "We must have disturbed him while he was having this tapir for supper. Have to be one hell of a cat to bring down an animal this size."

"Maybe we should keep going in case he's still around," Ramon suggested.

"Not a bad idea," Bolan agreed. "Let's move downstream about a kilometer before we stop to eat."

He glanced up at the dark sky, streaked with gold and pink. The sun was setting. The Executioner checked his watch. Almost 1830 hours. They had maintained a steady pace most of the day and covered roughly ten miles. Bolan's body was coated by a layer of sweat from the hours of hard labor. A cool breeze drifted across the rain forest like a balm to reward his efforts.

Bolan removed a small but powerful two-way radio unit from his pack. He pressed a button twice, which transmitted a signal to Grimaldi's gunship receiver that the mission was proceeding without need of assistance. A small amber light blinked in response to let

Bolan know the message had been received and the Stony Man pilot remained in radio contact.

The Executioner transmitted the signals only once every three to four hours. He wanted to keep radio contact to a minimum in case Valdez scanned frequencies with equipment sophisticated enough to realize someone was approaching his camp position. If Bolan pressed the button three times instead of twice, it would mean he had encountered a serious emergency and needed the pilot to come with the gunship for air support. He could transmit voice, but that would increase the possibility of being detected by enemy surveillance radio telemetry.

The trio moved along the muddy shore of the stream without encountering the jaguar or any other immediate threat other than swarms of hungry mosquitoes and deerflies. They headed into the trees, away from the sloppy mud and water that served as breeding areas for mosquitoes. Night had fallen when they found a suitable location to take a break.

They used a battery-powered hot plate to boil water for instant coffee and to heat rations. To sit on the ground and eat a warm meal seemed a luxury after the long hours of hard work and travel.

"Do you know when we will reach the terrorist camp?" Ramon inquired after they'd finished their meal.

"We're roughly halfway there," Bolan replied. "Judging from the topography of the maps, the rest of the journey should be easier terrain than what we've covered today. We should reach Valdez's base between 1630 and 2000 hours."

"I get confused by your military time," Raul admitted.

"Four-thirty in the afternoon to eight o'clock at night," Bolan explained. "The reason for such a difference in the time periods is bearing in mind we might encounter problems not on the map. Ideally we want to arrive a couple hours before sunset to do a recon before we set up our assault. We won't really know how many opponents we'll have to deal with or what sort of defenses Valdez might have until we see for ourselves. The more we know, the better our odds against him."

"I understand that," Ramon said, "but why sunset? I would think after midnight would be better so we could use the cover of darkness to our advantage."

"A couple reasons," Bolan answered. "By now, Valdez must suspect Arguello's team from the pier isn't coming back with or without that half million dollars. He knows there's a chance his base has been located and may be attacked. He'll increase security after dark. He and his people will be alert to danger. They've been at the site for a while and know the area. Cover of darkness will work in their favor as much as ours. Also, people tend to relax at sunset. The day is ending. Work shifts are coming to a close or are just about to begin. Evening meals are being prepared. Thoughts turn to relaxation, food and the next cigarette break, or to grudgingly accepting the start of a night shift. Such things distract a person from concentrating on security and remaining alert to danger.''

"Amazing," Raul remarked. "I never thought of it that way before, but I suppose you're right."

"Let's hope Valdez hasn't thought of it," the warrior said. "He's lost a couple rounds because we've been able to guess what he'd do, but don't underestimate the guy. He may be a fanatic, but he's still intelligent and cunning and certainly no coward. He's obviously willing to accept the hardships of living in a jungle environment. Probably takes pride in his Spartan life-style."

"You sound as if you respect him," Ramon commented.

"I respect any opponent who is potentially dangerous, but I don't respect him as a man because of the choices he's made. He could have accomplished something positive with such determination and leadership qualities."

"Really?" Ramon asked with surprise.

"If Valdez had come to Mexico to be a champion for the civil rights of the poor Indian class, he could have been a genuine instrument for reform and improved conditions for the less fortunate people in your country," Bolan stated. "Imagine a former member of an elite fighting unit from the U.S. military choosing to help really poor Mexican nationals in nonviolent protest against government policies of your country and mine. He would have been a much bigger embarrassment for the U.S. government because he would have appeared to be a concerned citizen, outraged by alleged exploitive actions and callous attitudes of U.S. policies toward Latin America."

"And we wouldn't be here now," Raul said.

"Valdez took a different path," Bolan stated. "His desire for bloody revenge hasn't done any good for anyone. His actions have gotten a lot of people killed and some more lives will be lost before this is over."

14

The three men continued to make their way through the rain forest in the dark. Thanks to Starlight goggles, which intensified reflected light to make the blackest night appear no more than dusk, the task wasn't as difficult or dangerous as it would have been for most travelers. They easily spotted a fer-de-lance by a fallen tree trunk and avoided the poisonous serpent.

Mack Bolan wanted to cover as much distance as possible to the enemy base, but he didn't intend to drive himself and his companions to exhaustion. They had pushed hard through the tough terrain with little rest. He knew, though, that fearful thoughts of a deadly confrontation with armed terrorists could rob his companions of badly needed rest. He wanted his three-man unit to get at least four hours' sleep and the twins would sleep more soundly if they were good and tired.

Bolan decided to set up camp when they reached the next natural landmark. The site would be ideal, a large clearing among a cluster of yucca caused by a lightning-induced fire during a thunderstorm. The clearing would eventually be replaced by new growth, but it would serve the Executioner's need for a bivouac area.

The brush required little use of their machetes to cut a path, and they didn't encounter any major obstacles in the night. The task seemed to be little more than a late hike, weighted down with gear and weapons.

Shapes suddenly appeared from the surrounding trees and ferns. Small, lean dark men seemed to materialize as if transformed from the vegetation by magic. Clad in handwoven clothing and straw sombreros, they all carried large jungle knives. Some held spears, others bows with quivers of arrows, and at least two had old double-barrel shotguns.

Local Indians, Bolan realized. They moved in the night like shadows, superb experts in stealth and camouflage. He held his M-16 at hip level, but held his fire. If the Indians meant them harm, they wouldn't have shown themselves.

Raul and Ramon stepped forward. Bolan wondered if the pair had lost their minds, but he figured he had to trust their judgment in the situation.

One of the Indians advanced and he spoke to the brothers in a language Bolan didn't recognize. The twins listened for almost a minute before they replied. The Executioner had no idea what they were saying. A few Spanish words popped up, but most of the conversation was conducted in a tongue that had no European origin. He glanced about at the solemn faces of the Indians. Bolan couldn't read any emotion in their features. He counted nine men, but suspected others could be hidden in the rain forest.

The man who appeared to be the spokesman pointed at Bolan and said something. Ramon turned to the Executioner and used the term "pacala" several times as he spoke. Bolan guessed this was what the brothers had decided to call him, but he had no idea what it meant.

A man stepped closer, holding a dead turkey by its feet. He offered the bird to the twins. Raul accepted the gift as Ramon searched his backpack and found several thick chocolate bars. The group chief took the candy, and the Indians departed into the rain forest, vanishing as quickly as they had appeared.

"We'll talk about this later," Ramon whispered to Bolan.

The Executioner nodded, aware it wouldn't be wise to converse in English within hearing of the Indians. They didn't speak until they reached the clearing by the yucca plants. White lily flowers supplied pleasant surroundings and an agreeable fragrance as the trio set up camp.

Raul raised the turkey. "This will be a good late supper and maybe an unusual breakfast as well," he announced.

"What was that all about back there?" Bolan asked.

"The men we met are Mayans doing a little late-night hunting," Ramon explained. "Mostly catch sleeping birds such as this turkey. They spoke a Yucatec dialect close enough to a language we know to allow us to understand one another.

"Knowing some Mayan legends has advantages," Ramon continued. "We told the chief we're descendants of the ancient Hero Twins. The Mayans were never a single empire, but most of them practiced a religion that included worshiping gods through their ancestor spirits. This means we're honored individuals of magical background."

"You seemed to be calling me by a name back there? Pacala?"

"Yes," Raul explained. "Pacala is an ancient Mayan term for 'shield' and refers to Jaguar Shield, who was a great warrior king, probably a foreigner from the north. We explained that you were the descendant of Jaguar Shield and you were with us to find and defeat some devils who had assumed human form. Sort of an exaggeration of the truth."

"Do they happen to know anything about Valdez and his gang?" Bolan asked.

"Of course," Ramon answered. "The Mayans know almost everything that goes on in the rain forest. They've been aware of the terrorists since Valdez set up his base, but this didn't threaten the Mayans so they didn't care. The Indians are more concerned about the *federales*, the military and the big business operations that threaten to destroy the rain forest and take their land. Valdez seemed to be fighting those forces, so the Mayans had no reason to object to him."

"I guess they wouldn't have much reason to, considering their point of view."

"That's why we told them the rebels in the center of the rain forest are really liars and evil spirits pretending to be their friends,'' Ramon explained. ''We told them that's why we had come, guided by the spirits of our honored ancestors, to find the enemy and destroy them. If we don't stop Valdez, the soldiers and the *federales* will come in large numbers. Government, and business with connections to government, will use the excuse to claim more land and cut down more of the jungle.''

''I suppose it's possible that really could happen,'' Bolan remarked. ''Things like that have happened in several countries in the past.''

''The chief said too many of the outsiders don't care about the way of nature or the cycle of life,'' Ramon said. ''He said everything—people, animals, plants— need the earth, the water, the air and the god symbols in the sky—the sun and the moon. The chief warned if outsiders keep taking everything from the earth for their own selfish, greedy reasons, and fill the water and air with poison, eventually the earth will die and the sun and moon will no longer look down on us with favor. If this happens, the chief said, all people will die, the outsiders as well as the Mayans.''

''Maybe he's right,'' Bolan replied. ''We didn't come here to save the world. We just came for Valdez.''

''We're headed in the right direction,'' Raul declared. ''The chief said the rebels have a village of 'canvas houses' with men and women, but no children.''

"That must mean tents," Bolan said. "Glad to hear there aren't any kids at the base. Did they say anything else about Valdez's camp?"

"The Mayans haven't actually gone into the base," Ramon answered. "The chief said the people there all seem to carry guns. Soldier guns for killing people, not hunting. They didn't want to get too close to the rebel village. The terrorists may be the enemies of the Mayans' enemies, but they're still outsiders. The chief said some of the people who are with Valdez come from Mayan villages, but they have assumed the ways of outsiders and he doesn't consider them real Mayans anymore."

"He said he hasn't been near the place for two *uinal,*" Raul added. "That's a type of month on a Mayan calendar, each twenty days long. Forty days ago is before the terrorist activity started. He said the other Mayans and other Indians in the area steer clear of the place."

"Good," Bolan stated. "I don't want any innocent bystanders in the line of fire when the shooting starts. But before that, we need to get some sleep. We'll take turns standing guard at two-and-a-half-hour shifts."

"First," Ramon said, "we'll eat the turkey they gave us. It might be the last meal for all of us, and we ought to enjoy it."

THE EXECUTIONER and the twins struck camp shortly after dawn. They had slept, and eaten roughly half the turkey. Well rested, bellies full, the men were ready for the final part of their journey. They checked their weapons and gear, sharpened the blades to their machetes and walked once more into the rain forest.

They soon discovered the trek became easier because brush, vines and large ferns had recently been cut and trampled by numerous jungle knives and booted feet. They even discovered a boot print left in a muddy patch of ground, about three days old. The waffle pattern suggested it was a military combat boot, and the depth of the print revealed the person who had stepped on the mud weighed about one hundred and thirty pounds.

"Valdez's people were through here," Bolan declared. "Maybe the group led by Arguello on their way to wherever they had the trucks to make the rendezvous with Farrel for the arms buy."

"We must be close," Raul said in a tense whisper.

"We have to get closer," the warrior replied. "Stay alert. If we encounter another human being from here on, he or she will probably be a terrorist."

They discovered more evidence of recent movement by many people through the jungle. A footpath had been worn into the ground, hidden beneath a canopy of tree branches. Bolan noticed they had entered a subforest of hardwood trees. According to the spy-satellite data, Valdez's base was located in the center of this area.

They approached a strip of tall grass that caught the warrior's eye because it hadn't been trampled like the rest along the path. He gestured with his machete to make Ramon and Raul stay back. Bolan approached the grass, knelt and carefully brushed his hand across the tips of the blades of grass. He peered down as he parted them and spotted a slender strand of fishing line running horizontally within the grassy strip.

"Trip wire," Bolan whispered. "Booby trap."

He followed the line and found one end tied to the roots of a hardwood tree. The other end disappeared among some ferns by the base of another tree. Bolan discovered a can firmly braced by rocks. A hand grenade was fitted inside, with the line and a bent fishhook attached to the ring pin. The can had been cut to make certain the spoon would pop free when the pin was pulled. Bolan guessed the pin had already been loosened so only a slight tug on the wire would trigger the trap.

The warrior grabbed the grenade to hold the pin in place and cut the line with a machete stroke. He carried the booby trap to the twins and showed it to them. Packed inside the can, surrounding the grenade, dozens of nails pointed from the mouth of the metal container.

"Extra shrapnel," Bolan explained. "The nails would be propelled by the grenade explosion. It would spray one hell of a wide pattern across this path."

Watchful for more booby traps, the trio continued, aware they were very close to the enemy base. They verified this when less than a hundred yards farther on they saw the terrorist camp through a curtain of ferns and tall grass.

Tents had been erected for the secret headquarters. Camouflage netting, laced with twigs and leaves, covered the tops of the tents, which explained why the camp hadn't been detected by military aircraft searching the jungles. The camouflage effectively broke up the shape of the tents and concealed them from view of passing planes and standard recon cameras. Branches and treetops of the hardwoods formed a ceiling over the entire base.

Valdez had selected an excellent site for his camp, Bolan realized. The tree cover not only hid the base, it provided a natural shield from the sun and damaging effects of heavy rainfall. A nearby stream provided plentiful fresh water, as well as fish, frogs, turtles and other food. Bananas, mangoes and other fruit could be gathered by the terrorists without attracting attention if they dressed in peasant garb instead of fatigues. They could hunt and trap birds, deer and other animals to supplement the supply of rations no doubt kept at the base.

A tower, with a hardwood framework, had been constructed beside one of the tents. Metal rods extended within the center of the tower to a platform at the top. Radio antenna, Bolan realized. The tent was the communications center for the base. A handrail around the platform revealed the tower could be used as a crow's nest to scan the surrounding area for possible danger.

The largest tents were probably barracks for the bulk of the terrorist troops, Bolan guessed, but he didn't have any idea how many men might be inside the canvas dwellings. More than a hundred could be housed in the tents, yet it was unlikely that many were packed into the camp. To have too many people residing in a small area would invite conflicts and quarrels. This situation could be dangerous with access to automatic weapons and explosives. Valdez would avoid overcrowding at his base. Besides, he had lost quite a few followers in the previous confrontations with the Executioner, and that had whittled down the population at the terrorist camp.

More than a dozen figures in fatigue uniforms were in view. Two were young women, seated on the ground, involved with conversation as they drank coffee and smoked hand-rolled cigarettes. Most of the males didn't appear to be working at any particular task either. A couple cleaned and oiled rifles. One guy, clad in cut-off pants, punched and kicked a heavy bag. Two others practiced free-spar fighting, a crude combination of judo, boxing and fundamental karate. However, they seemed to lack any real skill in these techniques. The match soon became a confused brawl as the combatants tried to wrestle wearing clumsy boxing gloves. A referee ordered them to stop as the pair rolled on the ground. They attempted to knee each other in the groin, hold with one hand and slug with the other and occasionally bite whatever target they could reach. Their martial-arts program seemed to be little more than practice at dirty fighting.

Bolan noticed a pair of men, armed with submachine guns, walking the perimeter of the base in an almost casual manner. The guards didn't appear to be concerned about the possibility of an attack on the camp at five o'clock in the afternoon. Good, the warrior thought. He hoped everybody in the place was as uninterested in security.

One of the smaller tents probably served as Valdez's head shed. The terrorist leader might be planning his next operation or trying to decide whether to abandon the site and move to a new area. He might even be asleep. Bolan wouldn't be surprised if the renegade tended to stay awake after dark. Valdez might be getting very paranoid and even distrustful of his own forces after so much had gone wrong with his terrorist schemes.

And it was going to get worse, Bolan thought as he studied the area. A stack of sandbags formed a semicircle around a long-barrel weapon with a bipod mount near the muzzle. Machine-gun nest, maybe an M-60 or something similar. Not good news for the Executioner and his allies. A big chain-fed weapon like that could fire close to a thousand rounds a minute and burn up hundreds of 7.62 mm shells without having to reload. One or two gunners could man the weapon and chop up a lot of surrounding jungle and any living thing along with it.

What other serious hardware did they have at the base? Bolan guessed they still had a supply of grenade launchers, explosives and perhaps rocket launchers as well. Such special weapons were probably stored in a tent that served as a type of arms room. Every terrorist had an automatic weapon, either at hand or within easy access. That alone gave them greater firepower than Bolan and the twins.

They had to hit the enemy with cunning and strike at targets to cripple the terrorists' defensive capabilities as fast as possible. Bolan figured he should station Raul in a good position to use his Marlin for effective sniper fire, and Ramon would need solid cover to lob grenades into the camp. They'd have the shotguns and revolvers for close quarters. The Executioner himself would have to take out the primary threats such as the machine-gun nest.

Bolan glanced about to determine the best locations for himself and the twins. Fortunately the hardwood tree trunks provided solid cover from virtually every angle around the base. The warrior prepared to signal to the brothers with hand gestures to send them to positions for a cross-fire attack, but movement within the camp caught his attention.

A man emerged from the tent next to the tower. His expression displayed concern and a sense of urgency. The guy carried two boxlike devices in his hands and gestured to some of the terrorists near the parade field at the center of the camp. He said something as he handed the objects to a pair of tough-looking young men.

"What's going on?" Ramon whispered. "What did he give those men? Walkie-talkies?"

"No," Bolan replied. "I've seen those things before. Those are the same type of motion or heat detectors used by Valdez's people at the Elizondo auto-repair shop when they came looking for me. Obviously they have some sort of detection security system set up in the commo tent.''

"So they know we're here," Raul said grimly.

"Yeah," Bolan answered. "Looks like we got a problem.''

15

The terrorists with the detection devices advanced, the high-tech divining rods held in one hand and weapons clutched in the other. The man who had been working out on a heavy bag padded forward on bare feet to ask what was going on. The combative pair ceased their awkward match and allowed the ref to remove their gloves, clearly too concerned with the possibility of a genuine threat from outside the base to want to continue their battle.

Both female terrorists rose, gathered up weapons and approached the men with the detectors. Several men also hurried forward. They gazed at the jungle, expecting to see whatever danger might lurk there. Two more men accompanied the pair with the devices as they advanced to the tree line. One of the women ran to the tower and started to climb for a bird's-eye view from the elevated platform.

Raul unslung the rifle from his shoulder. Bolan placed a palm on the barrel before the man could attempt to aim the Marlin. Raul looked at the Executioner as if he suspected the gringo had suddenly developed a death wish and wanted to take the brothers with him.

"Easy," Bolan urged. "They know something is here, but they don't know about us yet."

"You want to wait for introductions?" Ramon asked with a tense whisper.

"A heat detector or a motion detector may register large, moving warm-blooded objects, but it probably doesn't distinguish human beings from other mammals. If they had a system that sophisticated, they'd already be firing automatic weapons directly at us."

"So they might think we're just a friendly trio of jaguars strolling by?" Raul asked with a cynical snort.

"Or deer, tapirs, wild hogs or possibly a group of wandering Indians who've come across their base while hunting," Bolan explained. "These guys don't want to be on bad terms with the local Indians. If they get trigger-happy every time a detector spots something in the jungle, they'll run the risk of angering the Mayans or any other group that inhabits the area."

"So what do we do?" Ramon inquired. "Better be quick, or they'll be on top of us while we're still debating with one another."

Bolan spotted a fallen log near a cluster of ferns and grass. Several trees stood near the log. He formed a strategy as he hurried to the log and gestured for the twins to follow. They did so, not knowing what else to do. Bolan quickly removed his backpack and placed it and the M-16 behind a tree trunk.

"Get that gear off," he ordered. "Ramon, strip off your shirt and cap as well."

"*¿Qué...?*" Ramon began, baffled. "What is this?"

"You heard me. Do it."

"What do you have in mind, Mike?" Ramon asked.

The brothers followed orders. They reluctantly concealed their backpacks behind tree trunks as Bolan had done. Ramon pulled off his shirt and obviously felt uncomfortable and vulnerable in a thin white undershirt.

"Want to paint a bull's-eye on this as well?" he asked.

"Hide those shotguns too," the Executioner instructed. "Ramon, get behind the log. Make sure your pants are concealed by it. Then hang your upper body across the log and start to groan as if you've been injured."

"I don't like this," Raul announced.

"Neither do I," Ramon added.

"We're going to try to take these guys out quietly," Bolan declared. "The rest of the camp will be unsure what happened to their patrol and that will buy us a few minutes to get into position for our assault."

Bolan drew his machete. The brothers stared at the long steel blade. Raul pulled his jungle knife, but Ramon hesitated.

"I...I don't think I can kill a man that way," he admitted. "You have to get so close and...the blood..."

Bolan took the Beretta 93-R from shoulder leather. A nine-inch silencer was already attached to the threaded muzzle.

"You'll be exposed to the most immediate danger," he told Ramon, handing him the pistol. "Keep it hidden until you're ready to use it. I'll set the Beretta for 3-round bursts. Don't touch the trigger until you're going to shoot, and don't shoot unless you absolutely have to.''

Ramon nodded, accepted the handgun and went to lie down behind the log.

Bolan moved behind a tree trunk near the log, machete held close to his chest. Raul assumed a similar position by another tree trunk. The warrior inhaled deeply through his nose and drew the breath deep into his belly. He exhaled slowly, trying to calm himself and control the tension while he waited. The Executioner had lived with war his entire adult life, yet no sane man ever became immune to fear. Waiting for armed and deadly enemies to approach, while being forced to remain still, unable to see what the opponents were doing, was especially stressful.

He sympathized with the twins. Their experience at combat had been limited until this mission. Ramon and Raul were going through one hell of a baptism of fire. The role Ramon played at that moment was especially difficult. He had to act as bait, exposed to the enemy as he moaned and groaned in mock pain. The man sounded as if he really were hurt. Maybe he used the unintelligible groaning as a release valve for some of his fear.

Bolan didn't like putting another person in this sort of danger, but he couldn't play the role himself. The Executioner looked too Anglo, and he was too big to pretend to be a wounded Indian. Something could go wrong. The patrol might open fire the moment they saw Ramon and kill him on sight. Bolan wondered how Raul would react if the plan went badly and his brother died. Raul seemed the tougher of the pair.

That was why Bolan had guessed he would be willing to kill with cold steel at close quarters, but had doubted Ramon could do this—even before Ramon confessed it himself.

The warrior heard a slight rustle of cloth against leaves or ferns. The sound drew closer. The enemy had arrived. Bolan drew in a short breath and swung around the trunk, machete held in both fists. Bolan circled the tree in a single motion and found himself directly behind one of the terrorists.

The Executioner didn't hesitate. He swung the jungle knife and brought it down hard into the head of the enemy. Sharp, heavy steel chopped through bone, splitting the man's skull like a melon. Blood splashed Bolan's face and shirt as he turned his attention to his next opponent.

A startled face flashed in front of Bolan. The terrorist held a detection device in one hand and a .45 Colt pistol in the other. He tried to raise the latter, but Bolan delivered a karate hammer-fist stroke to the wrist above the pistol. Bone popped and the Colt slipped from limp fingers. Bolan's other arm bent and swung a frontal elbow blow to the side of his opponent's jaw. The elbow struck like a giant knuckle and spun the guy.

Once again behind an enemy, Bolan quickly took advantage of the situation. He wrapped one arm around the man's throat and clasped the other across the base of the terrorist's skull. With the forearm vise secure, Bolan stomped on the back of a knee to throw the man off balance and turned sharply. He heard bone crunch as vertebrae separated. The terrorist seemed to wilt in his grasp. He shoved the body aside, prepared to take on a third terrorist if necessary.

The harsh, sputtering cough of the silencer-equipped Beretta sounded. An enemy gunman toppled backward, his chest ripped by a trio of 9 mm bullet holes. Ramon held the 94-R in both hands, his arms braced across the log for a bench rest shooting stance.

Raul stood over the fourth and last member of the terrorist patrol. He had struck the enemy gunman more than once with his machete. Bloodstains streaked his torso.

Bolan glanced about for more terrorists, saw none and quickly moved to the corpse with his machete still jammed in its skull. He placed a boot on the dead man, gripped the handle and pulled hard. When the blade came free, the warrior wiped the jungle knife on the slain man's fatigues before he slid it back into the belt scabbard.

"Good work," Bolan announced. "Now, grab your gear and get into position as fast you can. We don't have much time."

"Won't they spot us with the heat or motion detectors in their radio tent?" Ramon asked as he rose on still-shaky legs.

"They might," Bolan replied, "but it doesn't matter. They won't know if what they register are members of a raiding unit or their own patrol. They wouldn't expect three guys to attack the base, so they'll probably guess the latter."

"Exactly," Raul agreed. "Who would think anyone to be that loco unless they met you, Mike."

"Sometimes being a little crazy can pay off," the warrior declared. "Get into position at the west flank, Raul. Over there."

He pointed to make certain Raul understood, gesturing to a pair of hardwood trees set close together at the south flank of the base.

"Ramon," he continued, "I want you over there. You both know what to do. Wait for me to get in position, and I'll fire the first shots or lob in the first grenade. That's your signal. We know there are more terrorists in the big barracks tents. I want you to concentrate grenade throws in that direction, Ramon."

"They'll throw grenades at us too," Raul remarked.

"You see anybody with a grenade shoot him or her," Bolan instructed. "Use that Marlin to pick off any target that isn't trying to surrender. Make sure you have good cover. If you change position, move farther into the jungle, not toward the base. Don't want anyone hit by friendly fire. Now, move!"

MOVEMENT AT THE FLAP of his tent startled Valdez. He grabbed the Heckler & Koch MP-5 and pointed it at the figure at the threshold. Perez stared at the muzzle of the submachine gun, his eyes wide with surprise and fear.

"You better announce who you are next time!" Valdez warned as he lowered the weapon.

"Someone or something is in the jungle near the camp," Perez said. "I thought you would want to know."

"What sort of movement was detected?" Valdez demanded. "How many are out there and where are they located?"

"I sent a patrol. They're not back yet, but they're searching the area with detectors."

"I didn't ask you if you sent anyone," the terrorist leader snapped. "Answer my goddamn question."

"I only detected movement made by three warm-blooded shapes the size of men or perhaps deer," Perez replied. "Probably just some Mayan hunters who wandered this way, but they could be a scouting team by the army of the *federales*. Maria climbed up the tower and didn't see anything, so there isn't a large attack force near the base."

"You should have told me about this immediately," Valdez complained.

He gathered up a bandolier loaded with magazine pouches for the H&K subgun and slung it across a shoulder. His machete was already in a sheath on his belt. Perez felt uncomfortable and confused by his leader's attitude. Valdez seemed too surly, too tense and angry to be making rational decisions.

Valdez marched from the tent and Perez followed. The terrorist leader discovered more than half the terrorist camp had assembled on the parade field. Some hadn't bothered to finish getting dressed in full uniform. Others fumbled with weapons, trying to load and chamber rounds. They stood in a confused cluster that didn't resemble a military formation.

"What is going on, chief?" a voice asked.

"I'm not some sort of magic man with magical powers of perception," Valdez replied. "I don't know any more than you at this point. Until we know otherwise, we have to assume the base is in jeopardy.''

A disturbed murmur erupted among the troops. Valdez shouted, ''Silence, you bunch of idiots!''

The crowd fell silent. Many appeared offended by the leader's insult, but Valdez didn't care if he lost any popularity contests. He couldn't trust most of them anyway, so it didn't seem to matter if they liked him or not.

''Rodriguez!'' Valdez yelled. ''Get twelve men and search the area. You find anybody who isn't one of our people, bring them in here for interrogation if you can. If you can't bring them back alive, kill them.''

''But if they're Indian hunter-gatherers—'' a female terrorist began.

''We can't take any chances,'' Valdez interrupted. ''They might be enemies in disguise or informers spying for the government.''

''The Indians have been willing to leave us alone and remain silent about us because they think our enemies are the same as those who threaten their lives and land,'' another member of the group began.

''Fuck those backward savages,'' Valdez rasped in English.

A number of the terrorists understood enough of the language to know what he said. Many of them were from Indian villages in or near the Yucatán, and were angered by Valdez's remark. More than one appeared tempted to turn their weapon on their leader.

''You'd better accept the fact we're fighting for our lives as well as for a cause,'' Valdez declared. ''You'd better realize we have no friends or family beyond this base. Forget old loyalties and be loyal to one another. You don't have a choice in this matter. It's too late to go back to your old lives."

"We didn't join you to turn against our own people!" an outraged voice announced.

"This is no time for these arguments!" Perez told them. "Before we do anything else we should make certain this camp is not about to be attacked by our enemies . . . the enemies we all agree threaten our people by their facist politics!"

"You mean like those who regard us Indians as savages?" a stocky terrorist of Mayan blood inquired as he waved his G-3 assault rifle toward Valdez.

A high-pitched whistle sounded above their heads. Valdez recognized the threat and hurled himself to the ground. He covered his head with his arms an instant before the grenade shell hit. The explosion roared from the center of the compound.

Screams echoed within the blast. Bodies and body parts were hurled across the base. A cloud of dust rolled over the dead and wounded. Valdez's ears rang, and his body throbbed from a pounding caused by being pelted by pebbles and debris. The terrorist leader got to his feet and gazed at the mangled remains of several slain followers.

"It's him!" Valdez exclaimed, spitting dirt from his mouth. "It's the bastard! I know it!"

"Chief," Perez said in Spanish, confused and rattled by the explosion, "I don't understand English...."

Valdez hadn't realized he had spoken English again. He had to keep his wits together. The base was under attack and the operation was coming apart. His people would panic if he didn't provide decent leadership in this crisis. Valdez switched to Spanish and addressed the man.

"Get your gun and take about one-third of what's left of our troops to cover the west and north flanks!"

"Yes," Perez agreed. "I'll put two men on the M-60 as well."

"Do it," Valdez agreed. "Make sure they're not stupid. We don't want them shooting down our own troops."

Perez dashed to the communications tent. Valdez pointed at the munitions tent and turned to Rodriguez.

"Get out the M-79 launchers!" he ordered. "Bring one to me and the other to someone who has been trained to use it. Break out the shells and distribute them as well."

Rodriguez nodded, ordered three terrorist troopers to accompany him and jogged toward the munitions tent. More terrorists began to emerge from the barracks tents. Another explosion brought one of the billets down in a heap of lumpy canvas. Figures struggled beneath the fallen tent. Blood seeped from the thick fabric, which revealed others hadn't survived the blast.

A rifle shot cracked, and Valdez saw one of his men whirl and drop. A ragged hole in the man's chest displayed the reason. The terrorist leader swung his H&K toward the surrounding rain forest, but he didn't know where the shot had come from.

Another projectile whistled from the sky. Valdez ducked for cover as the 40 mm grenade shell sailed into the base. The expected explosion occurred less than a second later, but the greater, far more powerful blast that followed caught the terrorists off guard. A violent shock wave seemed to ride through the ground beneath Valdez as if the explosion might trigger an earthquake.

He turned to see the munitions tent was gone. Only a charred crater and strips of burning canvas remained. Cartridges popped and spit out projectiles as flames ignited them at random. Valdez saw no sign of Rodriguez or the trio he had taken to get the grenade launchers, but Valdez knew what had happened to them.

"Where are you, you bastard?" Valdez cried out in rage.

MACK BOLAN BROKE OPEN his M-79 launcher and removed the spent casing of the 40 mm cartridge grenade. The weapon not only resembled a cut-down single-barrel shotgun with a huge bore, it was virtually designed like one. The Executioner had used such launchers many times in the past, even during his first tour of duty in Vietnam. The M-79 was outdated by modern warfare technology, but it could still get the job done under the right circumstances.

There was something to be said in favor of deadly simplicity, Bolan thought as he inserted another shell in the breech and snapped the weapon shut.

Another hand grenade exploded and brought down the second billets tent within the enemy compound.

Ramon was carrying out his part as planned. Bolan couldn't tell if Raul's sniper shots with the Marlin rifle had scored accurate kills, but he felt confident the other twin was also handling his job with equal efficiency.

The assault seemed to be going in their favor. That clustered congregation at the parade field had offered an unexpected prime target for the Executioner's first M-79 round. He had exploited the opportunity with lethal results. When he spotted four enemies headed for one of the smaller tents, Bolan guessed it might be the munitions center. His second 40 mm package proved he was correct, and the explosives stored there had caused greater havoc throughout the base.

Terrorists returned fire wildly. Bullets sprayed the rain forest in all directions. A few slugs struck the tree trunk Bolan used for cover. The lack of concentrated fire meant they hadn't accurately guessed his position. However, he knew if the enemy could bring the machine gun nest into action they would be able to sustain constant strafing fire. This would increase the chances of hitting Bolan or the twins and allow the terrorists to advance.

The Executioner moved to the cover of another large tree. He needed to get a better view to aim the M-79 at the machine-gun nest. He saw two figures by the wall of sandbags around the M-60. Just in time, Bolan thought as he raised the elevated sights to the M-79. He aimed with care, canted the thick barrel and squeezed the trigger. The weapon recoiled forcibly against his thigh, and a 40 mm projectile streaked high above the camp and descended directly in front of the sandbags.

The explosion tore the bags apart, ripped into the would-be machine gunners and sent the M-60 gun hurtling from the nest. The barrel was bent and the receiver smashed by the blast. One more major threat in the enemy camp had been taken out.

Bolan prepared to reload the M-79 when movement among the ferns and bushes near the perimeter of the base warned of danger. The warrior set down the launcher and unslung his M-16 assault rifle. He thumbed the selector switch to full auto and put the plastic buttstock to his shoulder.

The bush stirred again, but the warrior held his fire. He scanned the area for more opponents, aware that some of the terrorists were Indians. He recalled how stealthy the Mayans had been the night before. Hopefully anyone who had joined Valdez's extremist group had already spent enough time away from the role of hunter-gatherer in the traditional manner to lose some of these qualities.

An outline of head and shoulders appeared among some ferns. Bolan triggered the M-16 and a 3-round burst of 5.56 mm slugs smashed into the exposed cranium of the enemy. He immediately swung the M-16 toward the second telltale movement. Another terrorist rose with a submachine gun in both hands. He had moved directly into Bolan's sights, and the warrior drilled him through the heart with another trio of high-velocity bullets.

The second terrorist fell from view. Suddenly a rifle barrel poked between the stems of a yucca plant less than three yards from Bolan's position. The Executioner realized he couldn't bring his own assault weapon to bear fast enough to point and fire before the enemy could get off a shot. He ducked behind the tree trunk as his opponent's gun loosed a burst. Bullets sliced air near Bolan and chipped bark from the tree.

At least one hardman had obviously retained some of the superior arts of camouflage and stealth of the Yucatán jungle people. Not quite good enough, however, or the would-be killer wouldn't have exposed the gun barrel or would have concealed it by wrapping vines and twigs around the metal. The guy had made a mistake, but Bolan couldn't afford to do likewise.

He drew the .44 Desert Eagle from hip leather, held it in one fist and the M-16 in the other. The warrior thrust the barrel of the rifle into view. A salvo of automatic fire responded. The black plastic forearm stock shattered, and the impact of bullets yanked the assault weapon from his hand.

Bolan swiftly swung the Desert Eagle around the trunk and fired into the gunman's position. A high-pitched shriek announced a hit. The Executioner triggered the big pistol and blasted a second .44 Magnum round into the shape that abruptly sprang from the yucca. He glimpsed long black hair and fine features. Blood stained the fabric of a T-shirt over a bullet-punctured breast. The female terrorist tumbled downhill as Bolan lowered his pistol.

"Sorry, lady," he muttered. "You chose the wrong side."

16

Raul shoved fresh cartridges into the tubular magazine of his Marlin lever-action rifle. He had exhausted the original ammunition, but nearly each shot had brought down an opponent. His brother and the mysterious Anglo commando had effectively leveled the base with grenades. Yet another 40 mm shell crashed down into the center of the compound as he reloaded the Marlin.

That was the fourth M-79 round, Raul realized. The last "Señor Belasko" had packed for the mission. The American would have to rely on hand grenades and his other arsenal of firearms. Ramon had apparently exhausted his supply of grenades because he had switched to shooting the fearsome Beretta pistol at the enemy.

Raul saw his brother crouched by a tree, trying to take out a pair of advancing terrorists with the 93-R. Ramon hadn't removed the silencer, and this caused an unforeseen problem. The metal cylinder at the end of the barrel rendered the front-sight useless, and Ramon wasn't familiar enough with the pistol to compensate for that. The sound suppressor also reduced the velocity of the 9 mm rounds, so both range and accuracy were reduced.

Fortunately the report of the silenced pistol was muffled and the suppressor also concealed much of the muzzle-flash. Ramon didn't hit his intended targets, but the enemy couldn't detect his position by sight or sound. Frustrated, Ramon discarded the Beretta and reached for his pump shotgun.

Raul decided his brother might need him for backup. He darted from cover of the trees, knees bent and head down to use the concealment of a row of bushes as he ran. Raul's attention alternated between the enemy and his brother. He barely glanced down, and he had forgotten about the booby trap they had encountered earlier.

His boot stepped on a patch of brown, dead grass. It collapsed under his weight, and his foot plunged into a hole and pushed through something fitted inside it. He lost his balance and stumbled as piercing pain ripped into his ankle and calf. Raul hit the ground and cried out. Bone grated as the ankle was dislocated at the joint. His leg burned with agony as he rolled over and sat up as best he could.

Raul tried to pull his foot free and the stabbing pain increased. A scream nearly escaped his clenched teeth. He leaned forward to look into the hole. Raul gasped when he discovered the interior was lined with sharpened sticks. Several wooden points had impaled his leg. The pant leg and top of the combat boot were soaked with his blood.

How to free his foot presented a problem. Raul would probably tear it off on the spikes before he could pull it out of the hole. He considered smashing the sticks with the butt of his Marlin, but realized his reaction was inspired by panic. He needed something better suited for the task. Raul unsheathed his machete and carefully slipped the blade between the rim of the hole and his trapped leg.

Footfalls suddenly pounded toward Raul's position. He had almost forgotten about the terrorists. Three figures charged from the enemy camp. Raul reached for his holstered revolver as he stared up at the trio. He recognized the tallest man among the fanatics. Adolfo Valdez stood only two meters from the injured Raul.

"Found one of my punji-stick leg traps, huh?" Valdez remarked as he pointed his Heckler & Koch at Raul.

Raul pulled his .38 in a desperate effort to survive. Valdez triggered the MP-5 and blasted Raul from navel to throat with a burst of 9 mm slugs. Valdez watched his opponent flop against the ground in a violent spasm and nailed him in the chest with another short burst.

"Come, Chief!" a companion urged. "You already killed this one!"

Valdez spit on Raul's corpse and joined his two companions as they sprinted into the rain forest. Ramon saw the end of the exchange and witnessed the death of his brother at the hands of Valdez. He shouted Raul's name and swung the shotgun at the fleeing assassins. Ramon fired the weapon, but the terrorist commander and his accomplices were out of range.

Ramon began to give chase and jacked the pump to his shotgun. He had been so upset by his brother's death, he didn't realize he had exposed himself to the terrorists still located near the ruins of the base. A hot copper-clad projectile hit him in the left hip. Bone smashed, and the blow struck with sledgehammer force to knock Ramon to the ground.

The pain seemed to spread across his torso and threatened to rob him of consciousness. Ramon shook his head and gripped the shotgun in both hands as if hoping this would help him hang on to life. A shape approached the fallen Ramon and uttered an ugly, cruel laugh. The terrorist held a Browning pistol in both hands and slowly lowered the muzzle to point at Ramon's chest.

The fallen man raised the shotgun barrel and triggered the weapon, more instinct than deliberate action. Buckshot slammed into the terrorist and hurled his body backward before he could fire his pistol. Ramon surprised himself when he took out the killer, but his victory was short-lived as he heard another hardman approach. He fumbled with the pump action of the shotgun, aware he was taking too long to eject the spent shell and feed another into the breech while in the awkward position on his back.

A shot rang out. Ramon closed his eyes and stiffened before he realized that if he had heard the shot the bullet wasn't going to hit him. He craned his head forward as best he could and saw another terrorist had collapsed less than a meter from his feet.

The enemy gunman hadn't dropped dead from a heart attack. Ramon searched the rain forest and spotted the American. The big gringo held his .44 Desert Eagle in a two-hand Weaver combat grip.

"Mike!" Ramon called out. "Valdez killed Raul! He headed that way!"

He pointed with the shotgun to show the direction. Bolan jogged forward, still watchful of possible danger although the shooting had stopped. The entire terrorist compound had been destroyed, and its members were either dead or running for their lives.

"Don't waste time with me!" Ramon urged. "I can't run after the bastard, but I'll be all right! Just get him. Don't let him get away!"

"Don't worry," Bolan assured him.

The Executioner headed in the direction Valdez had fled. He moved quickly, no longer weighted down by the backpack and the majority of his weapons. Bolan had exhausted his supply of M-79 shells and abandoned the launcher. His M-16 had been smashed by bullets, the barrel bent and unreliable. Ramon still had his Beretta 93-R, but Bolan held the powerful .44 Magnum.

There was no time to scoop up an additional weapon from one of the dead terrorists. Valdez knew the area better than Bolan. If the man could get deep into the jungle, he would have a better chance of getting away or setting up an ambush to try to trap the Executioner.

The terrorist leader had chosen an easy route into the rain forest. The path had been previously cleared, and a foot trail had been worn into the ground. Naturally he wanted to get far away as fast as possible. Valdez wouldn't move to denser foliage until he had put some distance between himself and the battle-field.

This made following Valdez simple enough for Bolan. He ran at double-time pace, knees bent and body low to present a smaller target. He sidestepped a patch of discolored grass that appeared suspicious. Bolan guessed it might be a booby trap of some sort. He heard the rustle of movement in the brush and knew he was getting closer.

The warrior slowed his pace, aware the enemy could hear him as well. He advanced with caution and saw two figures by a column of hardwood trees and yucca bushes. The taller of the pair ejected a spent magazine from a submachine gun and reached for an ammo pouch in a belt slung across his shoulder. The other man held a G-3 assault rifle as he glanced about the rain forest, anticipating danger from all directions.

The Executioner stepped forward and dropped to one knee, his pistol trained on the enemy rifleman. The terrorist swung his weapon toward Bolan and tried to adjust the aim for the target's low position. The warrior triggered the Desert Eagle and blasted a single .44 Magnum round through his opponent's chest. The gunman fell backward, the rifle spinning from his grasp.

Valdez stared at Bolan as he held a full magazine of 9 mm rounds in one hand and the unloaded MP-5 in the other. The Executioner pointed the Eagle at the terrorist boss as he rose slowly.

"Go ahead, Valdez," Bolan told him. "Load that piece and chamber a round. I'll hold my fire until you're ready."

Valdez clucked his tongue with disgust and tossed down the weapon and magazine. He raised both hands to shoulder level and stepped forward. Bolan kept his pistol aimed at the renegade's torso.

"You want to kill me?" Valdez asked.

"I don't object to the idea," Bolan replied.

A crooked smile crept across Valdez's face as he stepped closer. "You would have shot me already if you didn't mind killing an unarmed man," he remarked.

"You want to bet your life on that?"

"I remember you at the embassy," Valdez said. "You were the one I saw on the hill at the auto-repair shop too. Isn't that right?"

He moved closer as he spoke. Bolan didn't bother to answer his question.

"Who the hell are you?" Valdez asked. "You must be one crazy bastard to come after me this way. Who are you working for? The CIA?"

"Who I am doesn't matter," Bolan answered. "You know why I came for you, Valdez. You can stand trial or you can die here in this jungle. Either way is okay with me."

"Do you know why I came to Mexico?" Valdez asked as he inched closer.

"Take one more step and you're dead," Bolan warned.

"I'm dead if you kill me or they send me to prison again," Valdez replied. "We're both soldiers. Killing and dying is part of our trade."

The yucca bushes suddenly parted. Perez emerged, an Obregon .45-caliber pistol in his fist. The communications officer didn't appear comfortable with a gun in his hand. He started to aim the weapon at Bolan and opened his mouth to say something.

Bolan swung the Desert Eagle toward the new threat, snap-aimed with the skill and instinct born of years of training and combat experience. He fired the Desert Eagle before Perez could trigger the gun or utter a word. A .44 Magnum slug entered the man's open mouth and blasted an exit at the base of his skull.

Valdez lunged as Bolan tried to bring the Eagle around in time to stop him. Steel flashed. Valdez swung his machete at Bolan's gun hand. Metal clanged on metal as the big knife struck the frame of the Desert Eagle and sent the pistol hurtling from the warrior's grasp.

Bolan jumped back to avoid another machete stroke and grabbed the hilt of his own jungle knife. Valdez slashed for the warrior's neck as the Executioner drew his machete and raised it high. The blades clashed and Bolan whipped a roundhouse kick to Valdez's ribcage. The blow staggered the terrorist and knocked him three steps backward.

"You really fucked up now!" Valdez snarled.

He slashed his jungle knife in a fast figure-8 pattern as he advanced. Bolan gripped the handle of his machete with both hands and stood his ground. Valdez cut another 8 with his weapon, and the Executioner stepped in and delivered a fast stroke while his opponent's blade was performing the pattern. Valdez cried out with pain and surprise. He jumped back, startled by a long cut across his chest. Blood seeped from the renegade's shirtfront.

Valdez raised his knife as if to deliver a chop, suddenly lunged and thrust the point of his blade toward Bolan's belly. The warrior slapped the flat of his blade across the attacker's machete to parry the stroke. He quickly caught the wrist above Valdez's weapon with his left hand and turned sharply. The action increased the terrorist's forward momentum and sent him hurtling into the trunk of a tree.

A groan announced Valdez's impact with the hardwood. Bolan rushed forward and swung his machete to try to end the lethal contest with a final stroke. Valdez whirled and lifted his weapon in a rising block. The blades clanged together once more. Valdez lashed out a high kick and slammed the outer edge of his boot to Bolan's forearm. The blow jarred the ulna nerve, and the warrior's fist popped open. The machete fell from his fingers.

Valdez pushed his advantage and moved in a circle to drive a left hook to Bolan's face. His fist caught the warrior on the cheekbone and drove him back two feet. The terrorist leader slashed his machete in a deadly stroke aimed at Bolan's head.

The Executioner sidestepped the attack, the blade slicing air inches from the warrior's shirtsleeve. He grabbed Valdez's arm with both hands before the terrorist could attempt another cut. Bolan stomped a boot into Valdez's right kneecap. Bone crunched in the joint, and the renegade cried out as the knee dislocated.

Bolan held on to the wrist with one hand to control Valdez's knife. The other hand whipped a back fist to the center of Valdez's face. Blood spurted from the guy's nostrils, and his head recoiled from the blow. Bolan still held the wrist and followed the back fist with an elbow stroke that caught his opponent on the point of the chin.

Valdez stumbled, dazed and barely able to stand on his shattered leg. Bolan swiftly grabbed his opponent's machete blade by the unsharpened steel spine with both hands. Valdez raised his left fist for a punch, but the Executioner thrust his head forward to drive a hard butt to the terrorist's battered face. Teeth cut his forehead as he slammed it into Valdez's mouth. The guy's head rocked back from the blow.

Bolan shoved with both hands and pushed the machete in a high, crescent arch. He shoved the sharp edge under Valdez's jaw and across the exposed throat, crimson pouring from the terrible, deep wound.

The terrorist's knees buckled and he dropped to all fours. An ugly liquid gurgle escaped from his slashed throat. His head dangled like that of a puppet with the strings cut. Finally his body slumped forward to lie facedown.

"Part of the trade," Bolan remarked, breathing heavily from the ordeal.

He pulled the two-way radio from a pocket and pressed the key three times to signal Grimaldi. Bolan inhaled and exhaled deeply to release stress before he spoke into the radio.

"Belasko to Grissim. Do you read me? Over."

"Read you loud and clear," Grimaldi replied. "On my way to your location. How's your situation? Over."

"Mission accomplished. Our bad boy is out of business. I got one wounded and one KIA. Over."

"Sorry about the bad news about the brothers," Grimaldi stated. "How about you? Over."

"I'm okay," Bolan assured him. "Be glad to get the hell out of here and head for home. Over."

"Hang in there," the pilot urged. "I'm tracking your signal and I'll be there soon. Does the colonel need to send in choppers to bring back any prisoners? Over."

"Not necessary," Bolan replied. "They ought to come in and clean up later, but all they'll need are a lot of body bags. Over."

"Over and out."

The Executioner located his Desert Eagle, picked it up and headed back to where Ramon lay, to wait for the chopper to arrive.

Take
4 explosive books
plus a
mystery bonus
FREE

Mail to: Gold Eagle Reader Service
3010 Walden Ave.
P.O. Box 1394
Buffalo, NY 14240-1394

YEAH! Rush me 4 FREE Gold Eagle novels and my FREE mystery gift.
Then send me 4 brand-new novels every other month as they come off
the presses. Bill me at the low price of just $14.80* for each shipment—
a saving of 12% off the cover prices for all four books! There is NO extra
charge for postage and handling! There is no minimum number of books I
must buy. I can always cancel at any time simply by returning a shipment
at your cost or by returning any shipping statement marked "cancel." Even
if I never buy another book from Gold Eagle, the 4 free books and surprise
gift are mine to keep forever.

164 BPM ANQY

Name _____ (PLEASE PRINT) _____

Address _____ Apt. No. _____

City _____ State _____ Zip _____

Signature (if under 18, parent or guardian must sign)

* Terms and prices subject to change without notice. Sales tax applicable in
NY. This offer is limited to one order per household and not valid to
present subscribers. Offer not available in Canada.

AC-94

A perilous quest in a hostile land

JAMES AXLER

DEATH LANDS®

Emerald Fire

In EMERALD FIRE, Ryan Cawdor and his band of warrior survivalists emerge from a gateway into an abandoned U.S. military complex, now a native shrine to the white gods of preblast days. Here the group is given royal treatment, only to discover that privilege has a blood price.

In the Deathlands, you're always too far from home....

When Remo and Chiun put their skills on the auction block, CURE is going...going...gone!

THE Destroyer

#101 Bidding War

Created by
WARREN MURPHY
and RICHARD SAPIR

Budget cuts are every administrator's nightmare, but CURE's own Dr. Harold Smith has a real whopper. A battle over bullion prompts Chiun to seek better pastures, and he's dragging Remo along.

Look for it in November, wherever Gold Eagle books are sold.

**Don't miss out on the action in these titles featuring
THE EXECUTIONER®, ABLE TEAM® and PHOENIX FORCE®!**

The Arms Trilogy

The Executioner #61195	SELECT FIRE	$3.50 U.S.	☐
		$3.99 CAN.	☐
The Executioner #61196	TRIBURST	$3.50 U.S.	☐
		$3.99 CAN.	☐
The Executioner #61197	ARMED FORCE	$3.50 U.S.	☐
		$3.99 CAN.	☐

The Executioner®

#61188	WAR PAINT	$3.50 U.S.	☐
		$3.99 CAN.	☐
#61189	WELLFIRE	$3.50 U.S.	☐
		$3.99 CAN.	☐
#61190	KILLING RANGE	$3.50 U.S.	☐
		$3.99 CAN.	☐
#61191	EXTREME FORCE	$3.50 U.S.	☐
		$3.99 CAN.	☐
#61193	HOSTILE ACTION	$3.50 U.S.	☐
		$3.99 CAN.	☐
#61194	DEADLY CONTEST	$3.50 U.S.	☐
		$3.99 CAN.	☐

(limited quantities available on certain titles)

TOTAL AMOUNT	$
POSTAGE & HANDLING	$
($1.00 for one book, 50¢ for each additional)	
APPLICABLE TAXES*	$_____
TOTAL PAYABLE	$_____
(check or money order—please do not send cash)	

To order, complete this form and send it, along with a check or money order for the total above, payable to Gold Eagle Books, to: **In the U.S.:** 3010 Walden Avenue, P.O. Box 9077, Buffalo, NY 14269-9077; **In Canada:** P.O. Box 636, Fort Erie, Ontario, L2A 5X3.

Name:_____

Address:_____ City:_____

State/Prov.:_____ Zip/Postal Code:_____

*New York residents remit applicable sales taxes.
 Canadian residents remit applicable GST and provincial taxes.

GEBACK11